# Doggy Stage Fright!

*That must be Lola's cue*, Nancy thought.

She saw Bess at the end of the runway, waving a biscuit high. Lola's ears perked up. But instead of walking toward the biscuit, she just looked at it!

The audience stared at Lola.

"Come on, Lola!" Nancy whispered. "Work it!"

Bess waved the biscuit faster and faster. George ran over to help. She snapped her fingers to get Lola to come. But Lola stood frozen, like a big white poodle statue!

Nancy gulped.

Something was wrong. Terribly wrong!

# Join the CLUE CREW
## & solve these other cases!

# NANCY DREW
## AND THE CLUE CREW

#6

## The Fashion Disaster

BY CAROLYN KEENE

ILLUSTRATED BY MACKY PAMINTUAN

Aladdin

New York London Toronto Sydney New Delhi

❦ ALADDIN

An imprint of Simon & Schuster Children's Publishing Division

1230 Avenue of the Americas, New York, NY 10020

First Aladdin Paperbacks edition February 2007

This Aladdin edition July 2015

Text copyright © 2007 by Simon & Schuster, Inc.

Illustrations copyright © 2007 by Macky Pamintuan

All rights reserved, including the right of reproduction in whole or in part in any form.

ALADDIN is a trademark of Simon & Schuster, Inc., and related logo is a registered trademark of Simon & Schuster, Inc.

NANCY DREW and related logos are registered trademarks of Simon & Schuster, Inc.

NANCY DREW AND THE CLUE CREW is a registered trademark of Simon & Schuster, Inc.

For information about special discounts for bulk purchases, please contact Simon & Schuster Special Sales at 1-866-506-1949 or business@simonandschuster.com.

The Simon & Schuster Speakers Bureau can bring authors to your live event. For more information or to book an event contact the Simon & Schuster Speakers Bureau at 1-866-248-3049 or visit our website at www.simonspeakers.com.

Designed by Lisa Vega

The text of this book was set in ITC Stone Informal.

Manufactured in the United States of America 0615 OFF

10 9 8 7 6 5 4 3 2 1

Library of Congress Control Number 2006929352

ISBN 978-1-4169-3485-1 (*The Fashion Disaster* pbk)

ISBN 978-1-4424-5909-0 (*The Fashion Disaster* eBook)

ISBN 978-1-4814-6075-0 (*Case of the Sneaky Snowman* and *The Fashion Disaster* proprietary flip-book)

# CONTENTS

# ChAPTER ONE

## Pampered Pup

"It's like a real, live fashion show!" eight-year-old Nancy Drew said to her two best friends.

Bess Marvin and George Fayne smiled and looked down at a pug dog on a leash. He was dressed in striped overalls and matching doggy booties.

"Except in *this* fashion show the models have four legs instead of two." Bess giggled.

It was Saturday, the day of the Cool Canines Fashion Show in River Heights Park. Mr. Drew had driven the girls to the park and agreed to meet them by the fashion show stage before showtime. Nancy was extra excited because

1

her Labrador puppy, Chocolate Chip, was a model in the show.

"Isn't Chip totally stylin' in her doggy denim outfit?" Nancy asked. "It's from the Funky Fido Boutique."

George bent down to straighten Chip's cap. "Chip looks totally fetching," she said. "Fetch . . . dog . . . get it?"

Bess rolled her blue eyes. "That's the fifth dog joke today, George," she said. "One more and I'll start calling you Georgia!"

"No, thank you!" George said, tossing her dark curls. She hated being called by her real name.

As the girls walked through the park, Nancy couldn't believe her eyes. The park looked so festive! Colorful balloons fluttered from a long runway built just for the fashion show.

"Do you think dogs like wearing clothes?" George asked. She was more into booting up computers than picking out new boots. But her cousin Bess was the total opposite.

"Who doesn't like new clothes?" Bess asked. She twirled to show off her yellow jeans and daisy print top. "Check out my new spring outfit."

"It's nice," Nancy said. "But aren't you afraid of getting dog hairs on it?"

"Dog hairs? I laugh at dog hairs!" Bess said. She reached into her pocket and pulled out a hairbrush. It was wrapped with tape, sticky side up.

"What is that?" George asked.

"It's my Hairy Fairy Wand!" Bess said. "I built it to pick up dog and cat hairs from clothes and furniture."

"Sweet!" Nancy said. She was proud of her two friends. Bess could build or fix anything. George was a computer whiz and proud of it. All three of them were great at solving mysteries. They had even started their own detective club called the Clue Crew. But today wouldn't be about cracking cases. It would be about walking on the runway!

"Look!" George said. "There's something you don't see every day."

Nancy turned to see where George was pointing. A bright-pink trailer was parked under a tree. Written on the side in fancy silver letters was the name LOLA.

"Isn't Lola that poodle who models for cards and calendars?" Bess asked. "The one they call the Diva Dog?"

"That's the one," Nancy said. "I heard Lola's the star of the fashion show today."

"That's *superstar*!" a voice piped up.

Nancy's reddish blond hair whipped in the air as she spun around. She saw two girls standing there, and sitting on the ground between them was Lola—the famous Diva Dog!

The big white poodle was dressed in a pink chiffon skirt and cape fastened with a pearl collar. She also wore a sparkly tiara on her furry head.

"It's Lola!" George exclaimed.

"May I pet her?" Nancy asked.

"Don't even think of it," said one of the girls,

who had wavy blond hair. "Lola just had a raw egg shampoo!"

"And a manicure!" the other, red-haired girl said. "Don't forget about the manicure, Maya."

"Like, duh, Nicki!" Maya groaned. "I'm the

one who picked out her cotton-candy pink nail polish, remember?"

Nancy glanced down at Lola's paws. The poodle really *was* wearing pink nail polish!

"Lola is *my* dog," Maya said. "My parents let me take her to fashion shows, photo shoots, pawtograph signings—"

"Pawtograph?" Nancy asked.

"Lola signs her pictures with her paw print," Nicki explained. "You know, autographs . . . pawtographs."

Maya and Nicki introduced themselves. They were in the third grade, just like Nancy, Bess, and George. The girls lived in the next town, Valley View.

"My name is Nancy," Nancy said. She pointed to Bess and George. "And these are my friends—"

*BZZZZZZ!*

The noise made Nancy jump. It came from Nicki's watch.

"Twelve fifteen," Nicki said. "Time for Lola's vitamin water break!"

Nicki pulled a bottle of water from her purple backpack and put it to Lola's mouth. She held it steady as Lola slurped loudly.

"Nicki is Lola's personal assistant," Maya whispered. "She can't have her own dog because her brother is allergic. So being around Lola is the next best thing."

Just then a gray, fuzzy-faced dog scampered over. He was wearing an orange vest that read "Adopt Me." Nancy guessed the dog came from the Rollover Rescue Shelter. The shelter had set up a tent in the park for the day.

Chip and the dog touched noses. But when the fuzzy-faced pup walked toward Lola, Maya screamed, "A shelter dog! Get him away from Lola! Get him away!"

The little gray dog scooted in and out between Nancy, Bess, and George's legs. The girls laughed and shrieked.

"Percy! Sit! Stay! Heel! Cool your jets!" A boy wearing an orange T-shirt ran over. Nancy thought he looked about nine years old. The boy tried to catch Percy but with no luck.

"We've got him!" a voice called.

Two teenagers wearing the same orange shirts as the boy raced over. Nancy read their name tags. The teenagers were Tracey and Vincent. The younger boy's name was Rusty.

Tracey pointed her finger at Percy. Then, in a firm voice, she said, "Sit!"

Percy stopped in his tracks and sat down, just like magic!

"Good boy," Vincent said.

"Wow!" Nancy said. "You guys are great with dogs!"

"That's because we're the Bow-Wow Brigade," Vincent said with a smile. "We volunteer for the Rollover Rescue Shelter. We feed dogs, walk them, clean their cages—"

"Ew!" Bess put in. "I hate cleaning out the hamster cage at school."

"I don't mind," Rusty said. "Before this, I volunteered at another pet shelter in Valley View."

"Valley View?" Maya said. "There is no pet shelter in my town. And no shelter dogs, either!"

"Huh?" Rusty said, wrinkling his nose.

"What's wrong with shelter dogs?" Vincent asked.

"The dogs we rescue are great," Tracey said.

"They're okay, if you like mutts and junkyard dogs," Maya said. "My Lola is a purebred standard poodle from the south of France!"

"Yeah . . . and I'm Spider-Man," Rusty muttered.

The Bow-Wow Brigade and Percy walked away. Nancy could tell they didn't like what Maya said about shelter dogs.

"We'd better go too," Nancy said. "Chip is

in the fashion show later, and I'm walking her down the runway."

"Lola walks down the runway all by herself," Maya bragged. "As long as Nicki waves her favorite dog biscuit."

"Chip has a favorite biscuit too," Nancy said. "It's called Lick My Chops."

"Shh!" Maya hissed. "Don't mention those yucky biscuits in front of Lola. She hates them!"

"Lola only eats Bone Appetit biscuits," Nicki said. "They're from a fancy pet bakery in New York City."

Nicki pulled a biscuit from her purple backpack. Nancy, Bess, and George jumped back. The biscuit smelled like stinky cheese!

"Lola's favorite flavor is blue cheese and onions," Maya explained. "She can smell them a mile away!"

George squeezed her nose and said, "So can we."

"Here. Give this to Lola," Nicki said. She tossed a biscuit to Bess. "Then you can tell everyone you fed the famous Diva Dog!"

Bess scrunched her nose as she caught the stinky biscuit. "That's okay," she said. "I don't really have to—"

"Arrf!" Lola jumped at the biscuit, her paws landing on Bess's shoulders.

"Lola—no!" Nicki said.

Nancy gasped. Bess's brand-new daisy top was covered with muddy paw prints!

# CHAPTER TWO

## Diva Dog Shocker

"Oh, no!" Bess cried as Lola jumped down, crunching the biscuit. "My new daisy top!"

"Are you lucky or what?" Maya said. "Now you'll have Lola's pawtograph all over your shirt!"

Nancy couldn't believe her ears! "Lucky?" she said. "Bess's new shirt is ruined."

"And Lola has the worst dog breath I ever smelled in my life," Bess muttered.

"Lola didn't mean it," Maya said with a smile. "But I know how I can make it up to you."

"How?" Bess asked glumly.

"Why don't you wave Lola's dog biscuit in the fashion show today?" Maya said.

"But I thought that was Nicki's job," Bess said.

"It *is* my job!" Nicki agreed.

"Not today, Nicki," Maya told her.

Nicki's face turned about as red as her hair.

"Fine!" she snapped. "I am sick of being a maid to that diva dog, anyway. Whatever Lola wants—Lola gets!"

Chip barked after Nicki as she stormed off.

"Nicki said 'diva' like it was a bad thing," Maya said with a shrug. She turned to Bess. "Well? Will you do it?"

"I don't know," Bess said slowly.

"Go for it, Bess!" George exclaimed.

"You'll get to be in the fashion show," Nancy said. "Just like Chip and me."

Bess's eyes lit up. Finally she smiled and said, "Okay. I'm in."

"Neat!" Maya said. "Lola's Bon Appetit biscuits are in a basket inside her trailer. My mom and dad filled it with fresh ones about a half hour ago."

"Are your parents in the trailer?" Nancy asked.

"No," Maya said. "They're at the mayor's lunch party in the park rec hall right now."

"My mom is there too!" George said. "She's a caterer. She cooked veggie lasagna and double-chocolate brownies for the party. I hope she brings home a doggy bag."

"Was that another dog joke?" Bess groaned.

Maya waved good-bye as she walked off with Lola.

Suddenly the loudspeaker crackled and an announcement blared. The fashion show would begin at one o'clock sharp.

"It's twelve thirty now," Nancy said, glancing at her watch. "We'd better pick up those biscuits."

"What if I can't find them?" Bess asked.

"You will," George said. "Just follow the smell!"

On the way to Lola's trailer, the girls saw kids from their school, River Heights Elementary. Ned Nickerson was walking his German shepherd, Max. Kevin Garcia was there with his beagle, Hudson. Andrea Wu was trying to stop her terrier, Angus, from chasing a squirrel.

But when the girls saw Peter Patino they had to stop and stare. Peter was walking a gigantic dog with thick black fur. A string of drool hung from the dog's mouth.

"Is that your dog, Peter?" Nancy called.

Peter stopped to give the dog a biscuit. "It's Mayor Strong's dog, Huey," he called back. "I'm just walking him while the mayor has his lunch party—whoaaaaaa!"

The dog barked as he dragged Peter away.

"It looks like Huey is walking Peter!" Nancy giggled.

The girls stopped to watch a clown make balloon animals in the shape of poodles. Then they remembered the biscuits, and they raced to the pink trailer and filed inside.

"Check out this place!" Nancy exclaimed.

Pinned to the wall were fashion photos of Lola. A fancy brass dog bed stood against the wall. Racks and shelves were filled with canine clothes and accessories. There was even a frilly vanity table that held bottles of doggy perfume!

"Now *this* is a doghouse!" George said.

"There's the basket!" said Bess. She ran to a brown basket that stood on a small table. Inside the basket were three dog biscuits. Nancy held Chip back as the puppy jumped at the treats.

"They don't smell so bad this time," Bess said. "Must be a different flavor."

George pointed to a sticky-looking puddle on the floor right next to the table. "Don't step in that," she said.

"Ew," Bess said, looking down. "I guess even diva dogs can have accidents!"

The girls left the trailer and ran straight to the fashion show runway. They checked in by the stage with Mr. Drew, and then Nancy and Chip lined up with the other owners and their dogs. Nancy saw a bulldog dressed as a cowboy, a dachshund wearing a leather jacket with silver studs, and even a Chihuahua in a hula skirt. But sitting like a princess at the front of the line was Lola the Diva Dog!

"Don't worry, Chip," Nancy whispered. "You'll always be top dog to me."

She was petting Chip when Mayor Strong and a woman walked by. Nancy recognized the woman with the dark hair and bright-red lipstick. Her name was

Patsy Ray, and she owned the Funky Fido Boutique.

"I still can't believe Lola is wearing that outfit," Patsy said in an angry voice. "I wanted her to wear one of my designs!"

"And I already explained it to you, Patsy," Mayor Strong said. "I promised Lola's owners she could wear an outfit from her new calendar."

Patsy's bone-shaped earrings swung back and forth as she shook her head. "Big mistake!" she said. "My clothes are so much cuter."

Then Patsy turned on her high heel and walked away.

*Wow*, Nancy thought. *And they call Lola a diva!*

Mayor Strong walked up the steps to the runway. The crowd cheered. Nancy's tummy fluttered like a million butterflies. She saw her dad out in the audience. It was showtime!

"I'm sure you're all excited to see Lola strut her stuff," Mayor Strong said with a smile. "But first let's welcome another superstar, Broadway actress Lorette Waters!"

Lorette waved as she joined the mayor on stage. "Thank you, Mayor Strong," she said. "Thank you, River Heights!"

Nancy listened as Lorette spoke about the importance of adopting homeless shelter dogs. Next the actress sang a song she'd written herself called "Send in the Hounds." As Lorette belted out the last stanza, she turned dramatically toward Lola.

*That must be Lola's cue*, Nancy thought.

She saw Bess at the end of the runway, waving a biscuit high. Lola's ears perked up. But instead of walking toward the biscuit, she just looked at it!

The audience stared at Lola.

"Come on, Lola!" Nancy whispered. "Work it!"

Bess waved the biscuit faster and faster. George ran over to help. She snapped her fingers to get Lola to come. But Lola stood frozen, like a big white poodle statue!

Nancy gulped.

Something was wrong. Terribly wrong!

# ChaPTER ThReE

## Sneaky Switcheroo

"Some diva dog!" Patsy Ray laughed from the stage. She was helping Lorette announce the show. "She can't even fetch a biscuit!"

Nancy frowned. Patsy Ray wasn't being very nice.

"Oh, well, folks," Lorette announced, "I guess even dogs get stage fright sometimes."

"Not this dog!" Maya shouted as she raced toward the runway. "Lola is a pro. A superstar!"

Maya grabbed the biscuit from Bess. She waved it herself—until she looked at it and shrieked.

"Waaaaa! This isn't a Bone Appetit biscuit, it's Lick My Chops!" Maya dropped the biscuit back into the basket and pointed to Bess. "And *she* switched the dog biscuits!"

"What?" Bess gasped.

Nancy was so surprised that she dropped Chip's leash. Chip barked and raced toward the basket of Lick My Chops biscuits. All the other dogs charged down the runway for the biscuits too—all the dogs except Lola!

"Angus, come back!" Andrea called.

"Hudson—bad dog!" Kevin shouted.

Dogs barked and whined as their owners

ran to catch them. Nancy had to jump over a dachshund to get at Chip.

"I didn't switch any biscuits!" Bess said over the noisy dogs and shouting owners. "I didn't!"

Nancy grabbed Chip's leash. She saw two grown-ups standing next to Maya. They had blond hair like Maya's.

"Mom, Dad, I know Bess did it," Maya said. "Lola jumped on her with muddy paws. So Bess got even by replacing the biscuits with the kind Lola hates!"

"You made that up, Maya!" George exclaimed.

"George and I were in the trailer when Bess picked up the biscuits," Nancy said. "She didn't switch anything."

"You're Bess's best friends," Maya said. "You probably *helped* her switch the biscuits!"

"We did not!" Nancy said.

Mayor Strong formed the letter *T* with his hands. "Time-out, everybody," he said. "Why don't we get some of Lola's favorite biscuits so she'll walk down the runway?"

"Because I don't want Lola in the fashion show anymore," Maya said.

"What?" the mayor cried.

"Lola is Maya's dog," Maya's mother said.

"So it's her call," added Maya's dad.

"But Mr. and Mrs. Milton," Mayor Strong reasoned. "All these people came to see Lola the Diva Dog!"

"They did not!" Patsy argued. "They came to see my fashions!"

"They came to adopt shelter dogs!" Lorette said.

"Can't we just have a fashion show?" George groaned.

The dogs and their owners lined up again—minus Lola. Nancy could see Lola's trailer zooming away. She couldn't believe Maya had accused all three of them of switching the biscuits!

"And now, after a little excitement," Mayor Strong announced, "the First Annual Cool Canines Fashion Show!"

Nancy tried not to think about Maya as she walked Chip down the runway.

"This is Chocolate Chip," Patsy said into the microphone, "looking cookie-sweet in her denim doggy ensemble—on sale now at the Funky Fido Boutique!"

The fashion show was a success even without Lola. Ned's dog Max needed some coaxing, but he walked down the runway like a pro. Andrea's dog got lots of laughs. And big Huey left a puddle of sticky drool on the runway.

When the show was over, Nancy ran over to Bess and George. They were helping Mrs. Fayne load her catering van. "That was fun, wasn't it?" Nancy asked.

"Fun?" George snorted.

"First my daisy top gets ruined," Bess said. "Now everyone thinks we switched those dumb dog biscuits!"

"No," Nancy said, shaking her head. "Just because Maya thinks that doesn't mean everybody does."

Just then two boys rode by on their scooters. One pointed at Nancy, Bess, and George.

"Hey, there they are!" one boy shouted. "Those are the girls who switched the dog biscuits!"

"Sneaky, sneaky, sneaky," the other said.

As the boys scooted away, Bess heaved a big sigh and said, "See what I mean?"

"Now what are we going to do?" George asked.

Nancy thought for a moment. There was only one thing for them to do. . . .

"We have to find out who really switched Lola's dog biscuits," she said.

"We?" Bess asked.

"As in the Clue Crew?" George chimed in.

"Sure," Nancy said with a smile. "We always help others by solving mysteries. It's time to help *ourselves*!"

# ChAPTER FOUR

## Trailer Bark

"Good morning!" Nancy said as she walked into the kitchen on Sunday.

"Morning, Sleeping Beauty!" Mr. Drew said. He was washing strawberries at the kitchen sink. Hannah Gruen was placing a plate of pancakes on the table.

Hannah had been the Drews' housekeeper from the time Nancy was three years old. She had helped take care of Nancy ever since her mother died.

Nancy smiled when she saw the yummy pancakes. But when she glanced at the Sunday newspaper on the table, she gasped. Splashed across the front page was the headline FAMOUS DIVA DOG FLIPS AT FASHION SHOW!

"Lola!" Nancy said.

"I read about that diva dog," Hannah said. "Why do you think she froze like that?"

"Somebody switched Lola's favorite dog biscuits on purpose," Nancy said. "The Clue Crew is going to find out who did it."

Mr. Drew popped a strawberry into Nancy's mouth. He was a lawyer and sometimes helped his daughter with her cases. "Sounds like an important case," he said. "Where are you going to start?"

Nancy caught a whiff of the pancakes and answered, "With a good breakfast, Daddy. Pass the maple syrup, please!"

After breakfast, Bess and George rang the doorbell. Then the Clue Crew ran up the stairs two at a time to Nancy's room, which was also Clue Crew Detective Headquarters.

"Okay. Let's get to work," Nancy declared.

George sat behind Nancy's computer. Her hands flew across the keyboard as she opened up a file for the case.

Bess plopped down on Nancy's bed. She tossed a stuffed unicorn up and down in the air. Throwing stuffed animals around was how she did her best thinking.

"First, let's come up with a time line," Nancy said. "When do you think Lola's biscuits were switched?"

"Maya said her parents had just filled the

basket with biscuits right before the lunch party," George remembered. "And the lunch party started at noon."

"If the party was at noon yesterday," Nancy said, "and we got to Lola's trailer a few minutes before the show—"

"Which started at one o'clock!" Bess cut in.

"That means," Nancy continued, "that the biscuits were switched between twelve and one o'clock."

"Write that down, George!" Bess said.

"What do you think I'm doing, Bess?" George joked as she typed. "Playing the piano?"

"Now that we have a time line, what about suspects?" Nancy asked. "Who would want to spoil Lola's big moment?"

"Probably someone who doesn't like Lola," Bess said. She began tossing a stuffed kangaroo in the air. "Or doesn't like Maya."

"What about Nicki?" Nancy said. "She was mad at Maya for giving her job to Bess."

"But where would Nicki get Lick My Chops

dog biscuits?" George asked. "She doesn't even have a dog."

"And all she fed Lola was that stinky kind," Bess said.

"Nicki had to get the Lick My Chops biscuits from somewhere," Nancy said. "In the meantime, she's a suspect."

George typed "Suspects," and underneath she wrote Nicki's name. Then Chip padded into the room. She was wearing the denim cap from the fashion show the day before.

"Chip looks so cute in Patsy's clothes!" Bess giggled.

"Patsy!" Nancy remembered. "She was arguing with Mayor Strong yesterday because Lola wasn't wearing the clothes she designed."

"Maybe Patsy switched Lola's biscuits," Bess said. "To make Lola look bad."

"Patsy Ray," George declared as she typed. "Suspect number two!"

"Two suspects but zero clues," Nancy said. "I wish we could go back and search Lola's trailer."

"How?" Bess asked. "We don't even know where to find it!"

"That's what *you* think!" George said.

She went online. After a bit of typing, Lola's own website came up. There was a picture of the poodle, surrounded by pink and silver stars. George clicked on the star marked "Meet Lola!" A page opened up, showing a list of Lola's appearances.

"Lola is signing pawtographs at the new pet store on River Street," George said. "Today at eleven-thirty!"

"Her trailer might be parked there too," Nancy said. "River Street, here we come!"

The girls each had the same rule: They could walk up to five blocks away from any of their houses, as long as they walked together and asked permission. River Street was less than five blocks away, so they were in luck!

When the three friends reached River Street, they spotted Lola's trailer. It was parked outside the new pet store, Ruffs and Meows.

Nancy, Bess, and George peeked through the store window. They saw Maya standing with Lola as kids lined up for her pawtograph.

Maya's mom stood outside. She was busy talking to a news reporter and a cameraperson. Lola's trailer was just a few feet away.

"The door is open," Nancy whispered. "Let's go!"

The girls slipped quietly into the trailer. Once inside, they scurried around looking for clues.

George studied the table where the basket used to be.

"If someone did switch the biscuits," she said, "what would they do with the Bone Appetits?"

"Maybe throw them away," Nancy guessed. She looked inside a small trash can, where she found shreds of paper.

"Somebody ripped up a note," she said. "That could be a clue."

Nancy never went anywhere without a pocket-size spyglass and plastic bags for her clues. She pulled a bag out of her pocket and filled it with the paper shreds.

"Look!" Bess said. She pointed to a framed picture on the wall. "It's Maya holding a poodle puppy. I'll bet it's Lola's baby picture!"

"We don't have time for that, Bess," George said. "We have to look for clues before—"

"—Mom!" a voice called from outside.

The girls froze.

It was Maya!

"I'm just going inside the trailer to get something, Mom," Maya's voice said next.

"Oh, no!" Bess gasped. "She's coming!"

"What do we do?" George whispered.

"We have to hide," Nancy said. "Right now!"

# ChAPTER FiVe

## Clothes Call

"Hide? Where?" George said.

The girls quickly looked around the trailer. Nancy spotted a large wire dog crate. Draped over it was a satiny blanket.

"Lola's crate," Nancy whispered. "There's room in there for all of us!"

"Gross!" Bess groaned.

The girls crawled inside.

Nancy gulped as she sat on a rubber steak dog toy that squeaked. George reached out to drape the cloth over the front of the crate. The girls held their breaths as the trailer door creaked open.

Nancy could hear Maya walking into the

trailer. She also heard a *click-click* sound—like dog paws on tiles.

"What a time to run out of pictures, Lola," Maya said. "Now where did I put your latest publicity photos?"

The girls were twisted inside the crate like pretzels. They heard Maya moving stuff around. Suddenly the *click-click-click* noise got louder and louder—as if Lola was walking toward the crate!

*Back, Lola, back*, Nancy thought.

Lola popped her head under the blanket and into the crate.

"Oh, noooo," Bess groaned.

After sniffing Bess's elbow and Nancy's sneakers, she began licking George's face!

George squeezed her eyes and mouth shut as Lola's tongue washed her face. Nancy hoped that George wouldn't yell out. But then Lola began licking George's mouth.

"Yuck! Ick! Phooey!" George yelled, wiping her mouth with both hands.

"Woof!" Lola barked.

One by one the girls spilled out of the crate. Maya stared at them as if they were from outer space.

"What are you doing here?" she demanded.

Nancy, Bess, and George all spoke at once.

"We're detectives!"

"We were looking for clues!"

"And the real person who switched the dog biscuits—"

"MOM!" Maya shouted.

"Maya—no!" Nancy said. "We can explain!"

Maya's mom peeked into the trailer.

"Guess what, honey?" she asked. "A nice television reporter wants to interview you with Lola. It's for the six o'clock news on WRIV-TV!"

"TV?" Maya said. A smile spread across her face.

"What should I tell them?" her mom asked.

"Tell them we're ready for our close-up!" Maya declared. She threw back her shoulders. Then she and Lola marched out of the trailer.

"I think I've seen you girls before," Maya's mom said. "Aren't you—"

"Lola's biggest fans!" George cut in.

"And we were just leaving," Nancy added.

"Bye-bye," Bess said.

The girls bumped into one another as they squeezed through the trailer door. As they ran down River Street, Nancy glanced over her shoulder. Maya was happily chatting to the reporter.

"That was close!" Nancy said when they slowed down. She pulled the plastic bag with the paper pieces from her pocket. "But we did pick up this clue."

"And dog hairs!" Bess said. She pulled out her Hairy Fairy Wand and swept it across their clothes. "I knew this would come in handy someday."

The girls talked about the case as they walked down River Street. With all its stores and places to eat, it was the busiest street in River Heights.

A woman walked by carrying a Funky Fido Boutique shopping bag.

"The Funky Fido Boutique is open today," Nancy said. "Let's go there and question Patsy."

The boutique was just down the block. Its window was filled with all kinds of dog clothes and accessories—sailor suits, hats, even angel wings!

"I don't get it," Bess said. "Why would someone

who designs such sweet dog clothes do something so mean?"

"She did say mean things about Lola," said George.

"Yeah, and I just thought of something," Nancy added.

"What?" Bess asked.

Nancy stared at her friends and said, "What if Patsy is mean to *us*?"

# ChaPTER Six

## Piece by Piece

"May I help you?" Patsy asked. Her back was to the girls as she hung fashion sketches on the wall. They were of dogs wearing ballet costumes.

"Why are those dogs wearing tutus?" George asked.

"I'm designing costumes for a doggy ballet called *The Muttcracker*," Patsy said. She turned around and peered over her red-framed glasses.

"Weren't you and your little dog in the fashion show yesterday?" Patsy asked Nancy.

Nancy gulped as she nodded. Then she gathered her courage and got right down to business.

"Patsy, do you remember when Lola wouldn't

walk down the runway yesterday?" Nancy asked.

"How could I forget?" Patsy said. "I laughed so hard my contact lens almost popped out."

The girls traded looks. Patsy was still saying mean things about Lola!

"Do you think you know who switched the biscuits?" Nancy asked Patsy.

"How should I know?" Patsy said with a shrug.

George stepped forward. "Then maybe you know where you were between twelve and one o'clock yesterday afternoon!" she said.

Patsy blinked hard. Then she smiled and said, "I'll take a wild guess. You girls are playing detective, right?"

"We're not playing, Ms. Ray," Nancy said.

"We *are* detectives," Bess added. "We're the Clue Crew!"

"You just gave me a super idea," Patsy said. She grabbed a sketchbook and began drawing on a fresh page. "I'll design detective clothes for dogs. Like tiny trench coats and those tweedy Sherlock Holmes caps—"

"Ms. Ray, please," Nancy cut in. "Can you tell us where you were yesterday?"

"Okay, let's see," said Patsy. "Yesterday between twelve o'clock and one o'clock I was at the mayor's lunch party. That's it."

Patsy turned back to her sketching. The girls began to whisper.

"She's acting like this is a big joke," Bess complained. "How do we know she's telling the truth about the mayor's lunch party?"

"I have an idea!" George declared.

She walked up to Patsy and said, "Ms. Ray? Do you recall what you ate at Mayor Strong's lunch party on Saturday between twelve and one o'clock?"

Patsy smiled for the first time, a big, bright smile.

"Sure do!" Patsy said. "I had the most fabulous vegetable lasagna. And for dessert I ate these scrumptious chocolate brownies. Double chocolate, I think."

"Vegetable lasagna and chocolate brownies are correct!" George declared.

Nancy smiled too. Patsy *was* at the lunch party. So she couldn't have been in the trailer switching the biscuits!

"I'll tell my mom you liked the food, Ms. Ray," George said. "She cooked all of it, you know."

"Your mom is a very good cook," Patsy said. Then she added with a wink, "And you girls are *awesome* detectives."

"Thank you!" Nancy, Bess, and George said together.

Maybe Patsy wasn't so mean after all!

The girls thanked Patsy and left the Funky Fido Boutique.

"Now our only suspect is Nicki," Bess said. "And we don't have a clue where she is."

"Clue!" Nancy gasped. "I almost forgot!"

She pulled the plastic bag from her pocket. Inside were the torn-up pieces of paper from the trash can.

"Let's put this note together and see what it says," Nancy suggested. "Maybe it'll give us some more leads."

The girls ran to an empty table in front of a café. Nancy poured the pieces out on the table. In a flash the girls were working at putting them together.

"It's just like a jigsaw puzzle!" Bess said.

As the pieces came together, George read the first words out loud: "MAYA . . . WE . . . KNOW . . . YOUR . . . SE."

"Se . . . Se . . ."

Bess thought out loud. "We know your seal! Your seahorse! Your set of crayons!"

George added the letter C.

"Sec . . . sec . . . secretary!" Bess shouted. "We know your *secretary*!"

"Bess," George complained. "Wait until all the pieces are together."

Nancy matched the last pieces:

R . . . E . . . T.

Then she read the message out loud: "MAYA. WE KNOW YOUR SECRET."

The girls traded looks. Secret? What secret?

# CHAPTER SEVEN

## Backpack Attack

"Maybe Maya's secret is something embarrassing," George said the next day. "Maybe she still sleeps with a teddy bear or something."

Bess planted her hands on her hips. "I sleep with a teddy bear!" she said. "And a dolphin, and a stuffed kitty with ruby eyes."

"Okay," George said. "Then maybe she bites her toenails."

"Ew," Bess said. "That I don't do!"

The girls were in the school yard for recess. But they weren't playing tag or kickball or swinging on the swings. They were trying to figure out the mysterious note. Nancy had taped it together when she got home the night before.

"The paper is orange with a dog paw-print design around the edges," Nancy said. "Whoever wrote it might like dogs."

"Nicki likes dogs," Bess pointed out. "And she probably knows some of Maya's secrets, too."

A ball rolled over. Nancy kicked it back to the kickball game. A girl wearing an orange T-shirt waved thanks.

Nancy's eyes flew open. The shirt made her remember the Bow-Wow Brigade. They wore orange T-shirts too!

"You guys," Nancy said, "didn't Maya say mean things about shelter dogs to the Bow-Wow Brigade?"

"Yeah!" Bess said. "Maybe they switched Lola's dog biscuits to get even."

"And while they were switching the biscuits," George added, "one of them might have stopped to write the mysterious note!"

"But what is Maya's secret?" Nancy wondered.

The end-of-recess bell rang. Nancy carefully folded the note and put it in her pocket. Then the girls lined up with the rest of their class. Their friends Nadine Nardo and Kendra Jackson stood in front of them in the line.

"Hi, Kendra," Nancy said. "Hi, Nadine."

Kendra and Nadine spun around to face Nancy. But they didn't say hi back. Instead they glared at the girls with squinty eyes.

"What's up?" George asked.

"We heard about it during recess," Nadine said. "How could you do that to Lola?"

"How could you switch her biscuits before the big fashion show?" Kendra asked. "That is so mean!"

Nancy couldn't believe it. Now their friends were blaming them for the biscuit brouhaha too!

"We didn't do it," Nancy insisted.

Kendra and Nadine hooked arms. With a huff they walked to the front of the line.

"Great," George groaned. "If we don't find out who switched those biscuits, we'll lose all our friends!"

Now Peter stood in front of the girls. He turned around and said hello.

"Hi, Peter," Nancy said. "Are you ever going to walk Huey again?"

Peter's eyes flew wide open. "Huey?" he asked. "Why do you want to know?"

"Just curious," said Nancy.

The line began to move. As they filed into the building, Nancy whispered to Bess and George, "Why was Peter acting so nervous?"

"Are you kidding?" George said. "You'd be nervous too if you had to walk a dog like Huey!"

The rest of the school day was busy with math, art, and social studies. But after three o'clock the Clue Crew was back on the case.

"Why is Chip coming with us to the Rollover Rescue Shelter, Nancy?" Bess asked.

Nancy held Chip's leash as they walked away from the Drew house. The girls had gotten permission to go to the Rollover Rescue Shelter after school.

"Because I have to walk Chip anyway,"

Nancy said. "Besides, since they like dogs so much, the Bow-Wow Brigade might be nicer to us if we have one!"

A rattling noise made Chip's ears perk up. Nancy turned and saw a girl riding a bicycle down the street. As she rode closer, Nancy could see who it was.

"It's Nicki," she said.

"Are we lucky or what?" George whispered.

"Nicki, stop!" Bess called, waving her arms.

Nicki smiled as she slowed down. Her purple backpack was stuffed in her bicycle basket. The strap from the bag dangled over the side.

"You guys were in the park on Saturday," Nicki said. "What's up?"

"We're trying to find out who switched Lola's dog biscuits at the show," Nancy said. "Maybe you can help us."

"Sorry," Nicki said. Her helmet wiggled as she shook her head. "I have no idea who did it."

Chip suddenly jumped up. She caught the strap of Nicki's backpack between her teeth.

"Chip—no!" Nancy scolded.

Too late. Chip pulled Nicki's backpack out of the basket. Stuff spilled out as it tumbled to the sidewalk. Nancy noticed a wad of gum stuck to a tissue, a dollar bill, a pencil with a

ladybug eraser, and a plastic comb.

"Sorry," Nancy said. But as she picked up the backpack, three more things fell out.

Three dog biscuits!

# ChAPTER EighT

## It's a Match!

Nancy grabbed Chip's collar as she lunged for the biscuits. They looked just like Lick My Chops!

"Where did you get those?" Nancy asked.

"They must be from Saturday," Nicki said calmly. "I forgot to clean out my backpack as usual."

"But they're Lick My Chops," Nancy pointed out. "When you fed Lola you only fed her the fancy kind."

"Those weren't for Lola," explained Nicki. "After I told Maya I quit, I went to the Roll-over Rescue tent to volunteer. Tracey gave me a bunch of biscuits to feed the shelter dogs."

Nancy watched Chip crunch the biscuits on the sidewalk. They were Lick My Chops all right!

"You can keep the biscuits." Nicki sighed. "I still don't have a dog."

Nicki adjusted her helmet and pedaled away. The girls stared down the block as she disappeared around a corner.

"How do we know she was telling the truth?" Nancy wondered.

"Too bad we don't have a lie-detector machine," George said.

"Maybe I can build one," Bess said. "Or invent a shampoo that makes a liar's hair turn green!"

"Thanks, Bess," Nancy said. "But we still have other suspects to question."

"The Bow-Wow Brigade!" Bess and George said together.

The Clue Crew went straight to the Rollover Rescue Shelter. Once inside they saw volunteers in orange T-shirts busy at work. They were walking dogs, cleaning cages, and showing adoptable dogs to possible owners.

Tracey and Vincent were there. When they saw the girls and Chip, they walked over.

"A brand-new puppy just came in," Tracey said.

"He's a schnoodle," Vincent said.

"A schnoodle?" Nancy asked.

"Part schnauzer, part poodle," Tracey explained. "Would you like to meet him?"

Nancy was curious about the schnoodle. But she shook her head and said, "We came to find out who switched Lola's dog biscuits before the fashion show."

Nancy pulled the note out of her pocket. She held it up and said, "We found this note in Lola's trailer. Did any of you write it?"

Tracey and Vincent stared at the note.

"That is our stationery," Tracey said. "But I didn't write it."

"Me neither," said Vincent with a shrug. Then he pointed to a desk. "If you'd like to volunteer, just write your name on the sign-in sheet and we'll put you to work."

The teenagers turned and walked away.

"Sign-in sheet," Nancy said. "That's it!"

"Don't tell me you want to volunteer now," George said. "We have a case to solve."

"And I'm *not* cleaning out any cages!" Bess said.

"You'll see," Nancy whispered. She waved her friends over to the desk. Then she ran her finger down the sign-in list until she found Tracey's and Vincent's signatures.

"What are you doing, Nancy?" Bess asked.

"Comparing the note to Tracey's and Vincent's signatures," Nancy explained. She held the note against the names and heaved a sigh. "The handwritings don't match."

"Somebody had to write that note," George said.

Nancy compared the note to each name on the list. Finally she found a match.

"Bess, George," Nancy said. "The volunteer

who wrote the note was that kid Rusty!"

"Did somebody say my name?" a voice asked.

The girls whirled around. Rusty was standing behind them. He was holding a leash in one hand and a bag of dog poop in the other.

"I was just walking Champ," Rusty said.

"We can see that," George said, wrinkling her nose.

"Rusty, did you write this?" Nancy asked, holding up the taped-together note.

"Here. Hold this," Rusty said. He handed Nancy the poop bag and took the note.

Nancy scrunched her nose as she looked down at the bag. Rusty studied the note. He nodded and said, "Yeah. I wrote this. So what?"

"It's not nice to leave creepy notes around!" Bess scolded.

"I know, I know," Rusty said. "But that Maya was making fun of shelter dogs. And shelter dogs are great!"

"Is that why you switched Lola's biscuits, too?" Nancy asked.

"No way!" Rusty said. "That would be going against the Bow-Wow Brigade Pledge."

"What pledge?" George asked.

Rusty spun around. Printed on the back of his T-shirt was the Bow-Wow Brigade Pledge. The first line read, "Never hurt or trick any dog."

"A pledge is a serious promise," George whispered.

"I took a pledge," Bess said. "When I joined the Pixie Scouts."

"Well?" Rusty said, turning around. "Now do you believe me?"

"I guess so," Nancy said.

"But what is Maya's secret?" Bess asked.

Rusty tossed the orange note on the desk. Then he flashed a sly grin. "It's not nice to tell secrets, either," he said. "Come on, Champ. Let's go."

The girls watched as Rusty walked away.

"Wait!" Nancy called. "You forgot your bag!"

"Now we'll never know Maya's secret," George said.

"And now Nicki is our only suspect," added Bess.

"Maybe, maybe not," Nancy said. She tossed the bag into a trash can. Then she flipped the pages of the sign-in sheet until she found the one from Saturday.

"Look!" Nancy said. She pointed to a name near the bottom of the list. "Nicki Weidemeyer," she read. "That's got to be the Nicki we know."

"So Nicki *was* telling the truth," George said. "She really did volunteer with the dogs on Saturday."

"Now we have no suspects," Bess said. "And everyone still thinks we switched the dog biscuits."

The girls left the shelter. On their way out they ran into Mayor Strong.

"Hi, Mayor Strong," Nancy said. "What are you doing here?"

"I'm on my way to the vet stationed here," Mayor Strong said. "To pick up a special toothpaste for my dog Huey."

"What makes it special?" George asked.

"It's superstrong," the mayor said. "Huey has had the worst dog breath since Saturday. Sort of like cheese and onions!"

"Cheese and onions?" said Nancy.

Mayor Strong nodded. "Now if I can just get Huey to stop drooling like Niagara Falls," he muttered.

The girls said goodbye as the mayor entered the building.

"Wasn't the flavor of Lola's favorite dog biscuits cheese and onion?" George asked.

"Mayor Strong said Huey's breath has been stinky since Saturday," Nancy said.

"The day of the fashion show!" Bess gasped.

Nancy smiled as the pieces in her mind began to click together.

"Maybe Lola's biscuits weren't switched," she said. "Maybe they were *eaten*!"

# ChAPTER NINE

## "Newfie . . . Goofy!"

"You mean Huey ate Lola's dog biscuits?" Bess asked.

Nancy nodded and said, "There were no crumbs, remember? A big dog like Huey could have eaten those biscuits in one gulp!"

"And when the basket was empty," George said, "Peter might have replaced them with the dog biscuits he had in his pocket."

"Which could have been Lick My Chops!" Nancy put in.

"But why wouldn't Peter say anything?" Bess asked. "He saw how everyone was blaming us."

"Because Huey is the mayor's dog," Nancy said. "And Peter was responsible for him."

"Maybe he was afraid to let anyone know," said George.

Nancy remembered how nervous Peter had acted in the school yard. No wonder he didn't want to talk about Huey!

"I do think Huey ate the biscuits," Nancy said. "But before we accuse him, we have to do a little research."

"Research on what?" George asked.

"On dogs!" Nancy replied with a smile.

The Clue Crew raced to their headquarters. George found a website about different dog breeds. They couldn't remember the type of dog Huey was, but they remembered what he looked like.

"That's him!" Nancy said. She pointed to a big black dog on the screen.

"That's a Newfoundland," Bess said, reading carefully. "Newfie for short."

"It says they used to help fishermen pull in their nets," George went on. "And that they love water."

"It also says Newfies drool in long, sticky ropes," Nancy added.

"Can you imagine having a dog like that?" said Bess. "He probably drools on everything—furniture, the floor—"

"The floor!" Nancy said. "Maybe that's what that sticky puddle in Lola's trailer was."

"You mean that was Huey's drool?" Bess asked. She scrunched up her nose. "What else does it say about Eww-fies, I mean, Newfies?"

George read out loud: "Newfies' coats have long black hairs. They shed often, too."

"I wonder if Huey left hairs in the trailer too," Nancy said.

"Wonder no more!" exclaimed Bess.

"Huh?" George said.

Bess ran to her jacket. She pulled her Hairy Fairy Wand from her pocket.

"I used this right after we were in Lola's trailer, remember?" Bess said. "Huey's hairs could be on it."

The Clue Crew examined the sticky white

tape on the Hairy Fairy. There were lots of light hairs— just like Lola's. There were also long, thick black hairs—just like Huey's!

"Maya and her parents have blond hair," said Nancy. "So the black hairs must be Huey's!"

"Good work, Gizmo Girl!" George said.

"Thanks!" Bess said.

"Let's question our new suspect," Nancy suggested. "Peter Patino."

Nancy found Peter Patino's address in the River Heights Elementary School yearbook. It was three blocks away.

When the girls reached the Patino house,

they found Peter in his front yard. Huey was also in the yard. He was sitting in a plastic kiddie pool, covered with soapsuds!

"Peter's giving Huey a bath," Bess whispered. "It's a good thing Newfies like water."

Peter stopped scrubbing as the girls walked over.

"Hi, Peter," Nancy said. "Hi, Huey."

The girls stepped back as Huey panted.

His dog breath *was* pretty funky!

"Mayor Strong asked me to wash Huey," said Peter. "It took four dog biscuits to get him into the bath."

"What kind of dog biscuits?" Nancy asked. "Lick My Chops . . . or Bone Appetit?"

Peter froze with his hands on Huey's wet coat. "I don't remember," he said. "Dog biscuits are dog biscuits."

"Not to Lola," George said. "Did Huey eat her fancy biscuits before the fashion show?"

"Nuh-uh," Peter said, shaking his head.

Nancy didn't always like tricking suspects

into confessing. But sometimes it was the only thing to do. . . .

"First Huey ate the biscuits," Nancy said. "Then he got muddy paw prints all over Lola's fancy dog bed. And after that, he ripped up some of Lola's clothes. Right?"

"Wrong!" Peter exclaimed. "All Huey did was eat those stinky dog biscuits—"

Peter clapped his wet hand over his mouth. A bubble floated out between his fingers.

"Tell us what happened, Peter," said Nancy.

Peter uncovered his mouth. Then he took a long, deep breath.

"After I saw you on Saturday, Huey dragged me into Lola's trailer," he said. "He's so strong that I couldn't hold him back—even when he started eating the biscuits from the basket!"

"*All* the biscuits?" Bess asked.

"To the last crumb!" Peter said. "I didn't know what to do, so I refilled the basket with my own dog biscuits. How was I supposed to know that Lola hated Lick My Chops?"

"Why didn't you tell someone?" George asked. "You saw how everyone blamed us."

"I was in charge of Huey," Peter said. "So when he goofed, I didn't want anyone to know. Especially since he's the mayor's dog. I'm sorry!"

"It wasn't your fault," said Bess. "Dogs will be dogs."

"You should tell Maya what you just told us, Peter," Nancy said. "Then maybe she'll stop blaming us for switching the biscuits."

"And start blaming me?" Peter said. "I don't think so!"

Huey barked. He jumped out of the pool and began shaking the water off his thick, wet coat. The girls and Peter screamed as they got showered.

"I think Huey is trying to tell you something," Nancy said.

Peter brushed back his wet hair with his hand. "Okay," he said. "Let's get this over with!"

Peter had seen Lola's trailer on River Street after school. When the kids reached River Street, it was still there.

"There's Maya!" Nancy said.

Maya and her mom were walking out of a pet photography studio. Maya held Lola's leash while her mom stopped to buy coffee from a cart.

"Maya!" called Nancy.

"Leave us alone," Maya called back. She walked Lola into the trailer. Nancy, Bess, George, and Peter followed them inside.

"I said leave us alone!" Maya warned.

"It's okay, Maya," Nancy said gently. "Peter Patino was at the park on Saturday. He has something to tell you."

"What?" Maya asked.

"We-ell," Peter started. He shuffled his feet. "It's sort of . . . like this . . . you see . . ."

George gave Peter a nudge with her elbow.

"Mayor Strong's dog, Huey, ate Lola's fancy dog biscuits," Peter blurted out. "While I was walking him."

"He did?" gasped Maya.

"I couldn't stop him," Peter said. "I'm sorry."

"Wow," Maya said. She looked at Nancy, Bess, and George. "So you didn't switch the biscuits. The mayor's dog ate them?"

"Yes," Nancy said.

Maya gave a little snort. "That sounds like something a dumb shelter dog would do. They're nothing but trouble."

Nancy frowned. She was glad the Bow-Wow Brigade wasn't around to hear that!

"I guess I'm sorry for blaming you," Maya

told the girls. "But you'd better go now. Lola has another photo shoot in exactly ten minutes."

"I'm outta here!" Peter declared. In a flash he was out of the trailer.

"We'd better go too," Nancy said.

Maya turned to Lola. She began brushing her coat with a silver-plated hairbrush.

The girls headed toward the door. Nancy glanced at Lola's puppy picture on the wall. It showed Maya holding a tiny white poodle in her arms. Nancy remembered seeing it when they were in the trailer before.

*Cute!* she thought.

She was about to follow Bess and George when she noticed something else. In the picture was a crate—the cardboard kind used to bring puppies and kittens home for the first time. Nancy wondered if the writing on the crate was in French, since Maya said that Lola was from France. But the print was too small to read.

*My spyglass!* Nancy remembered. She reached into her pocket and pulled it out.

"What are you doing, Nancy?" whispered Bess.

Nancy peered through the spyglass as she read the words silently to herself: "Valley View Pet Shelter. Next Stop: Home!"

"Bess, George!" Nancy gasped. "I think I just found out Maya's secret!"

# ChAPTER TEN

## Happily Ever After

Nancy held the spyglass as Bess and George looked through it. They read the words to themselves.

"Wow!" Bess said.

"No wonder Rusty knew Lola's secret," George whispered. "He volunteered at the Valley View Shelter!"

"What are you doing?" Maya called.

The girls turned to Maya.

"Question," Nancy said. "Is Lola a shelter dog?"

Maya froze with the hairbrush in her hand. Then she shook her head. "Shelter dog?" she scoffed. "Ha, ha, very funny."

"Then what's a shelter crate doing in Lola's puppy picture?" Nancy asked.

Maya's eyes popped open wide. She glanced at the picture and shook her head.

"The puppy in the picture isn't Lola," she said. "That's some Lola wannabe from the Valley View Shelter. We were giving her diva lessons and . . . and . . . and . . ."

Nancy folded her arms across

her chest. Maya's voice cracked as she tried again.

"I needed a crate for an arts and crafts project," Maya said quickly. "So I went to the Valley View Shelter and . . . and . . . and . . ."

Maya's eyes darted around the room. They finally landed on Nancy.

"Okay." Maya sighed. "My parents adopted Lola as a puppy at the Valley View Shelter. So I guess that does make her a—"

Maya gulped hard. She opened her mouth, but all that came out was a squeak.

"Go ahead. Say it," Nancy said gently.

"THAT MAKES HER A SHELTER DOG!" Maya blurted. "There! Are you happy now?"

Lola began licking Maya's face.

"Somebody seems to be," Nancy giggled.

"But why was it such a big secret?" Bess asked.

"Yeah," George said. "Adopting homeless dogs is a great thing."

"It started when Lola got famous," Maya

said. "I didn't think anyone would buy calendars and cards from a shelter dog. So I made up a fancy story to go with Lola's fancy life. I begged my parents to go along with it and they did."

Tears filled Maya's eyes as she petted Lola.

"Lola may be a French poodle," Maya sniffed. "But she's never even been to France. Not even to Paris, Texas!"

Maya buried her face in Lola's coat. She began to sob loudly.

"Don't cry, Maya," Nancy said. "Lola's story is even better now!"

"It is?" asked Maya. Her voice sounded muffled through Lola's fur.

"Sure," Nancy said. "Most people don't know you can adopt purebred dogs at shelters. Or puppies that can grow up to become superstars, just like Lola!"

Maya choked back the tears as she looked up.

"Don't you see, Maya?" Nancy went on excitedly. "Lola is just like Cinderella!"

"I get it!" George said. "It's like she went from wags . . . to riches!"

This time even Bess laughed at George's dog joke.

"Lola the Cinderella Dog!" Maya declared. She nodded her head. "I like it. I like it."

"So do I," Nancy told Bess and George. "Not only is Lola's secret out—but the Clue Crew solved another case!"

"It's just like a fairy tale!" Bess swooned.

Nancy, Bess, and George stood outside the Rollover Rescue Shelter. They gazed at Lola, dressed in a white lace doggy gown and silver tiara. She made the perfect Cinderella—and the perfect poster pup for Adopt-a-Shelter-Dog Day!

While the Bow-Wow Brigade walked adoptable dogs, Maya chatted with a news reporter.

"Is it true?" the reporter asked. "Did Lola the Diva Dog really come from a shelter?"

"Oh, yes!" Maya said. She looked straight

into the camera. "I guess you can say she went from wags to riches!"

"That was my joke," George muttered.

Peter came over with Huey on a leash. Nancy couldn't believe her eyes. Instead of pulling Peter, the big Newfie was walking calmly at his side!

"What happened to Huey?" asked George.

"When I told Mayor Strong about Huey and the biscuits, he decided to send him to obedience school," Peter explained. "Now Huey is an A student!"

"Way to go, Huey!" Nancy cheered. She jumped back before Huey could drool on her sneaker.

"Nancy, Bess, George!" a voice called.

Nancy turned. It was Nicki, walking a small pointy-eared dog on a leash.

"Look at my new dog!" exclaimed Nicki.

"I thought you couldn't have a dog because of your allergic brother," Nancy said.

"No problem," said Nicki. "Meet Enrique—a Mexican hairless!"

"I never met a bald dog before," Bess said.

"No hair, no sneeze!" explained Nicki.

"Wow!" George said. "I guess there is a dog out there for everyone."

Next came the moment the girls had been waiting for. Vincent, dressed like a fairy tale prince, got down on one knee as he fitted Lola with a crystal-clear doggy shoe.

"Glass slippers can be bought at the Funky Fido Boutique," Patsy Ray announced. "Get a pair for your princess pup while supplies last!"

Nancy turned to smile at her best friends. "This fairy tale had a happy ending," she said. "Thanks to the Clue Crew!"

"I guess we are good detectives," Bess said.

"Are you kidding?" George said with a grin. "We're *doggone* good!"

# Say Fleas!

Who says only divas get star treatment? Now your fave dog or top cat can get face time with their own picture frame, made and designed by YOU!

### You Will Need:
One picture of your pet

Acrylic paint

Fine-tipped marker

Arts and crafts glue

Paint brush

5-x-7-inch piece of plain cardboard

Pair of scissors or craft knife

Clear nail polish

Ribbon or magnet

## On Your Bark ... Get Set ... Go!

Place the picture of your pet in the center of the cardboard, and use a pencil to trace around the picture. Ask an adult to help you cut out a hole for the picture.

Glue dog biscuits or any solid pet treats to the frame. Add stickers, glitter, feathers—even your pet's paw print for extra pizzazz!

Use the marker to write your pet's name on one of the treats, then brush clear nail polish over the treats for a shiny finish.

When its dry, flip the frame over and glue your pet's picture on the back.

Glue a magnet or colorful ribbon on the back of the frame.

Wait for the glue to dry, then hang up and enjoy!

Don't forget—frames can be for the birds, too! Decorate a frame with jingly bells and colorful bird seed. It's sure to fly with your best feathered friend.

You always knew your pet was perfect. Now he's picture perfect!!

# Who is this cool ghoul?

*This really is a mystery,* Nancy thought. *Who could the Snowman be?*

Suddenly something big and white dashed out from behind a tree. A bright blue scarf fluttered from its neck as it darted from tree to tree.

"Yikes!" Nancy gasped.

"Nancy—are you okay?" Bess asked.

"Yeah," George said. "You look like you just saw a ghost!"

# Join the CLUE CREW
## & solve these other cases!

# NANCY DREW
## AND the CLUE CREW®

#5

## Case of the Sneaky Snowman

### BY CAROLYN KEENE

### ILLUSTRATED BY MACKY PAMINTUAN

**Aladdin**

New York   London   Toronto   Sydney   New Delhi

❤ ALADDIN

An imprint of Simon & Schuster Children's Publishing Division

1230 Avenue of the Americas, New York, NY 10020

First Aladdin Paperbacks edition December 2006

This Aladdin edition July 2015

Text copyright © 2006 by Simon & Schuster, Inc.

Illustrations copyright © 2006 by Macky Pamintuan

For information about special discounts for bulk purchases, please contact Simon & Schuster Special Sales at 1-866-506-1949 or business@simonandschuster.com.

The Simon & Schuster Speakers Bureau can bring authors to your live event. For more information or to book an event contact the Simon & Schuster Speakers Bureau at 1-866-248-3049 or visit our website at www.simonspeakers.com.

Designed by Lisa Vega

The text of this book was set in ITC Stone Informal.

Manufactured in the United States of America 0615 OFF

10 9 8 7 6 5 4 3 2 1

Library of Congress Control Number 2006922340

ISBN 978-1-4169-1254-5 (*Case of the Sneaky Snowman* pbk)

ISBN 978-1-4424-5914-4 (*Case of the Sneaky Snowman* eBook)

ISBN 978-1-4814-6075-0 (*Case of the Sneaky Snowman* and *The Fashion Disaster* proprietary flip-book)

# CONTENTS

# CHAPTER ONE

## Puzzle in the Park

"And now for the finishing touch!" eight-year-old Nancy Drew said. She held out her hand. "Carrot please, George!"

Nancy's best friend George Fayne dug into the pocket of her bulky blue parka. She pulled out something green and fuzzy. Then she stuck it into the face of the snowman with a *crunch*!

Bess Marvin was Nancy's other best friend. She stared at the fuzzy green thing with wide eyes.

"You were supposed to bring a *carrot* for the snowman's nose," Bess said.

"That's broccoli," Nancy said.

"My mom needed carrots for her catering

job," George explained. "Broccoli was the only veggie we had left."

Nancy smiled. It was Tuesday morning and the best winter break ever! That's because it had snowed for two days straight. By the time Nancy, Bess, and George got to the park it looked like a giant marshmallow sundae—perfect for building their first snowman of the year!

"Wait! Wait! We're not finished yet," Bess said. The pom-pom on her red hat bounced as she jumped up and down. "We forgot to *name* our snowman!"

"How about Sherlock?" Nancy asked.

"Sherlock?" George said, wrinkling her nose.

"After Sherlock Holmes, the famous detective in the books," Nancy explained. "We're detectives, so our snowman should have a detective name. Right?"

"Right!" Bess and George said together.

Not only were the girls detectives, but they had their own detective club called the Clue Crew. When a mystery popped up in River Heights, Nancy, Bess, and George were on the case!

The friends stepped back to admire their work. Sherlock had Nancy's old blue scarf wrapped around his neck. Over his head were earmuffs. Bess built them out of two white powder puffs and a plastic headband. George stuck a pair of her dad's old rubber boots near the snowman's base. For his mouth and smile, Nancy used little

round dog kibbles—the kind she fed to her puppy, Chocolate Chip.

"Did we do an awesome job or what?" Bess sighed.

"We?" George cried. "You mostly just watched, Bess!"

Bess rubbed her thick red mittens together to keep warm. "I told you. I'm skating in the River Heights Ice Spectacular Show this Saturday," she said. "I can't get my hands cold!"

"You're not skating on your *hands*, Bess," George said. She rolled her dark eyes. "Sometimes I can't believe you're my cousin."

Nancy sometimes couldn't believe it either!

George had dark hair and brown eyes. She was a computer geek and proud of it. Bess had blond hair and blue eyes. She loved building and fixing things. But now Bess had something else to look forward to. A few days ago she won a raffle at the ice-skating rink. The prize was to skate in the ice show with Russian ice dancing stars Svetlana and Alexi Dubonov. On Saturday

Bess would wear a pretty costume and ice skates with pink pom-poms. Then she would skate in the show like a star herself!

"It's okay, Bess," Nancy said. "You made Sherlock's earmuffs. That was a big job!"

Bess stuck her chin out at George. Suddenly someone shouted, "Wipeout!"

Nancy, Bess, and George whirled around. A boy was riding a snowboard down the hill—straight toward them! They jumped behind Sherlock and all held their breath as the boy zipped by.

"He almost rode into Sherlock!" George complained.

"And he didn't even say excuse me!" Bess said.

Nancy watched as the boy skidded to a stop at the bottom of the hill. He laughed as he picked up his board and walked away.

"Oh, forget about him," Nancy said. She pulled the zipper of her red parka all the way up to her chin. "Let's go to the Snack Shack for some hot chocolate."

"With marshmallows!" Bess added.

The girls said good-bye to Sherlock. Their boots made deep footprints as they walked through the snowy park. Tons of kids were busy sledding and building snow people. But as the girls passed the playground they saw something that made them stop. Between the slide and the swings was a purple and gold tent!

"That was never there before," Nancy said.

She looked closer. Eight-year-old Toby Leo was standing in front of the tent. Toby was in the girls' third-grade class at River Heights Elementary School. He usually wore a sweatshirt, blue jeans, and sneakers. But today he was wearing a fancy green turban and a gold cape!

"Wow," Nancy said. "Toby looks like someone out of the story 'Aladdin.'"

"So does that tent," Bess said. "But what's it doing on the playground?"

"I'll bet Toby is putting on some kind of play," George said. "Let's ask him."

As the girls walked closer Nancy saw a sign

pinned to the tent: HOT CHOCOLATE WITH MARSH-MALLOWS. $1.00.

"Are we lucky or what?" George said.

"Hi, Toby," Nancy said. "Can we have some—"

"Stop!" Toby said. He held up his hand like a school crossing guard. "You must wait your turn!"

The flap of the tent swung open. A girl burst out with a big smile. "Yes!" She pumped her fist.

"I'm going to be an astronaut when I grow up! I'm going to the moon! The moon!"

Nancy, Bess, and George traded puzzled looks.

What was going on in there?

Toby folded his arms across his chest. "Madame Coco Chocolata will see you now!" he announced in a deep voice.

"Madame Chocolata?" George whispered.

"Who is Madame Chocolata?" Bess whispered back.

Nancy stared at the tent. This was way too weird!

"I don't have a clue," Nancy said. She took a step toward the tent. "But there's only one way to find out!"

# CHaPTER TWO

## Snow Problem!

"Close the flap!" a voice cried. "It's freezing out there!"

The girls stooped to get into the tent. Nancy smiled when she saw their classmate Deirdre Shannon inside. Deirdre was sitting cross-legged on a blanket. She wore a gold turban, hoop earrings, and beaded necklaces over her down jacket. On the blanket was a thermos, a stack of paper cups, and a bag of mini-marshmallows.

"Hi, Deirdre!" Nancy said.

"What's up?" George asked. "Halloween was months ago."

"I am not this Deirdre you speak of," Deirdre

said. "I am Madame Coco Chocolata—teller of fortunes!"

"Fortunes?" Nancy, Bess, and George said together.

Deirdre's turban almost fell off as she nodded her head. "Some fortune-tellers read palms. Others read tea leaves," she explained. "But I, Madame Chocolata, read the marshmallows in hot chocolate!"

"Huh?" George said.

Deirdre picked up the thermos and smiled. "For just one dollar you get a steaming cup of cocoa," she said, "and your life's destiny."

Nancy glanced sideways at her friends. Deirdre Shannon always got whatever she wanted— which probably explained the fancy tent. But she was usually busy working on her website, Dishing with Deirdre.

"Whoever heard of reading marshmallows?" Bess whispered.

"She's got hot chocolate," George whispered. "Who cares what she does with it?"

"Thanks, Deirdre," Nancy said. "We'll each have a cup . . . and our fortunes!"

"And so you shall!" Deirdre said. As she poured hot chocolate into three cups, Nancy chatted about Sherlock.

"You should go and see him, Deirdre," Nancy said. "He's the best snowman ever!"

"Really? What does he look like?" Deirdre asked.

"You're the fortune-teller." Bess giggled. "You tell us!"

Nancy jabbed Bess with her elbow. Deirdre was taking this game very seriously!

"Sherlock has a blue scarf and a broccoli nose," Nancy said. "And he's right near the water fountain."

"Which isn't really a water fountain today because the water's frozen," George added.

Deirdre lined the white cups in a row. "Quick!" she said. "I must read your fortunes before my trance breaks. And before the mini-marshmallows melt."

The girls sat cross-legged in front of Deirdre.

"Madame Chocolata will read Nancy's fortune first," Deirdre said. She stared into a cup without blinking. "I see a pizza in your future. A large pizza with extra cheese. Madame Chocolata predicts pizza for dinner tonight!"

"If you say so," Nancy said. "But my dad only orders pizza on Saturday nights—"

"Next!" Deirdre said a little too loudly.

"That's me," George said. "What do you see in my hot chocolate? Am I going to get that neat computerized watch I want?"

Nancy smiled. George loved computers more than anything. She even had a computerized toothbrush!

"I see a snowman," Deirdre said slowly. She stared into the cup. "Near the water fountain."

"Ye-ah! We just told you that," George said.

"Wait!" Deirdre said. She leaned over as she stared deeply into George's cup. "The snowman is taking a long, long journey. He is walking . . . walking . . ."

George laughed and said, "Snowmen can't walk—"

"Next!" Deirdre cut in.

"Bess, that's you," Nancy said.

"This is too silly," Bess said, shaking her head. "I don't want to play. I just want a cup of hot

chocolate with marshmallows, please."

Deirdre narrowed her eyes at Bess. She waved her hands over the last cup of hot chocolate and said, "I see a big ice show! I see someone falling on the ice! And lots of people laughing and saying, 'What a klutz! What a klutz!'"

"What?" Bess gasped. "You mean I'm going to fall in the Ice Spectacular? With Svetlana and Alexi Dubonov?"

"It's in the marshmallows," Deirdre said with a shrug. "That will be three dollars, please. Have a nice day."

The girls dropped their dollar bills into a basket. They sipped their hot chocolate as they left the tent.

"Nancy, George!" Bess cried. "What if Deirdre really can see the future? She already knew I was in the show!"

"Who *doesn't* know?" George said. She licked a marshmallow from her upper lip. "You told practically the whole school. And the world!"

"Deirdre is just doing this for fun," Nancy

said. "Come on. I want to show you something."

The girls finished their hot chocolate as they
made their way over to Sherlock. Nancy pointed
to their snowman and smiled.

"See?" Nancy said. "Sherlock didn't take a
long journey like Deirdre said. He's still where
we left him."

Bess smiled and said, "You're right. I guess it
was kind of silly."

"If anyone is a klutz, it's me!" Nancy said. She
pointed to a stain on her scarf. "See? I already
dripped hot chocolate all over myself!"

The girls watched as a bird landed on the
broccoli nose. They giggled as he began peck-
ing at it.

"At least somebody likes broccoli!" George
said. "Let's go home now, before my toes turn
into toesicles!"

Nancy, Bess, and George left the park. They
all had the same rules. They could walk anywhere as long as it was no more than five

blocks from their houses. And as long as they were together.

"Let's come back to the park tomorrow," George said. "We can make snow angels and have a snowball fight."

"Maybe we can build a snow*woman*!" Nancy said.

"Okay," Bess said with a groan. "But from now on, let's bring our own hot chocolate!"

"Can people read fortunes, Daddy?" Nancy asked at the dinner table that night.

Mr. Drew shrugged as he poured dressing over his salad. He was a lawyer and great at figuring things out. "Some people say they do," he said. "They read palms. Or tea leaves. Or—"

"Marshmallows?" Nancy said.

"Did you say marshmallows?" Mr. Drew asked.

"Deirdre says she can read the marshmallows in hot chocolate," Nancy explained. "But it didn't work. She said we'd have pizza tonight—"

"And we're having vegetable lasagna!" Hannah

said as she carried a casserole dish into the dining room.

Hannah Gruen was the Drews' housekeeper. Hannah had been taking very good care of Nancy since Nancy was three years old. That's when Nancy's mother had died. Hannah brushed Nancy's reddish-blond hair every morning until it shined. She made the best tuna sandwiches with tomatoes. And Hannah always smelled like sugar cookies—even when she wasn't baking!

"Yummy!" Nancy said. She took a whiff of the hot steaming lasagna. "Who needs pizza when we can have this?"

Just then the doorbell rang.

"Who could that be at dinnertime?" Mr. Drew asked.

Nancy glanced at the clock in the dining room. It was six o'clock. Sharp.

Mr. Drew left the room to answer the door. When he came back he was holding a big flat box. "Did anyone order this?" he asked.

Nancy stared at the box. There was only one thing that came in a box like that!

"Pizza?" Nancy gasped. "No way!"

"Maybe Hannah ordered the pizza," George said. "To go with the lasagna!"

It was Wednesday morning. The girls were walking through the main gate of the park. It was so cold they wore layers of fleece shirts under their parkas.

"Hannah said she didn't," Nancy said. "She even called Pizza Paradise. They said someone ordered the pie at five thirty but didn't leave a name."

"Omigosh!" Bess gasped. "Madame Chocolata

said you'd have pizza for dinner and she was right!"

Nancy smiled as she shook her head. "Daddy and I figured it out," she said. "Deirdre probably ordered the pizza herself to make it look like her fortune came true."

"But I saw Deirdre at the mall yesterday," George said. "She was trying on shoes with her mother. And it was exactly five thirty."

"How do you know it was exactly five thirty?" Nancy asked.

George pulled up her sleeve to show a hi-tech silver watch. "Because I got the computerized watch I wanted," she said excitedly. "I couldn't stop looking at it!"

Nancy's heart sank. She'd thought she had the whole thing figured out, but she didn't.

"If Deirdre was trying on shoes at five thirty," she said, "then she couldn't have ordered the pizza."

Bess stopped walking. Her eyes flashed with fear.

"If Deirdre was right about the pizza then she'll be right about me," Bess said. "I'm going to fall on the ice in front of hundreds of people!"

"Right," Nancy chuckled. "And our snowman will take a long journey too!"

"As if that's going to happen!" George laughed.

Bess finally smiled too. "You're right," she said. "The only snowman who can walk is Frosty!"

The girls began singing "Frosty the Snowman." Their singing stopped when they reached the water fountain.

Nancy, Bess, and George looked around. Something was missing.

"Um . . . Bess, George?" Nancy said. "Where's Sherlock?"

# Chapter Three

## Snowball Fright

"Are we sure this is the right spot?" Bess asked.

"Totally," Nancy said.

The three friends stared at the empty spot in the snow—the spot where Sherlock had been standing just yesterday.

"Maybe he melted," Nancy said.

"He couldn't have melted," George said. "The temperature is still below freezing. And all the other snowmen from yesterday are still around."

"Then what happened to Sherlock?" Bess asked. "Did he take a walk? Just like Deirdre said he would?"

Nancy walked to the spot where Sherlock

had stood. She patted the snow on the ground. "Someone probably knocked him down," she said. "That's all."

"Then where is Sherlock's scarf?" George asked. "And his broccoli nose? And my dad's old boots?"

"I don't know," Nancy admitted. She saw a big footprint in the snow. Looking up she saw a whole trail of footprints leading away from the site.

"Look," Nancy said. "Whoever knocked down Sherlock left footprints."

George tilted her head as she studied a print. "The soles had a diamond design—just like my dad's old boots," she said. "The boots we put on Sherlock."

"Then Sherlock did walk away!" Bess gasped. "Just like Deirdre said he would."

Nancy shook her head. She didn't believe for a minute that Deirdre was a fortune-teller. There had to be a reason that Sherlock wasn't there!

"Hey, guys!" a voice called out.

Nancy turned. Their friends Marcy Rubin and Trina Vanderhoof were walking over. Trina's thick furry boots made loud clomping sounds in the snow. Marcy wore blue rubber boots with a pretty white snowflake design.

"Guess where we're going?" Marcy asked.

"To the beach!" George joked. "To swim with the polar bears and penguins!"

"Very funny," Trina said with a smirk. "We're going to see Madame Chocolata!"

 *Oh, no,* Nancy thought. *Not them too!*

"Trina and I saw Madame Chocolata yesterday," Marcy said.

"She told me I'd get a bright and shiny surprise."

"What did that mean?" Nancy asked.

"Ta-daa!" Marcy sang. She held up her wrist to show a bracelet with glittery pink beads. "This was in my mailbox this morning. Isn't it awesome?"

"Totally," Bess muttered.

"Madame Chocolata said I'd get a new basketball," Trina chimed in. "And this morning I found a basketball in my front yard! How cool is that?"

"Way cool," Bess muttered again.

"Who needs a magic eight ball when you have Madame Chocolata?" Marcy said.

"Her hot chocolate is pretty good too," Trina said. "Come on, Marcy. Let's see what's in the marshmallows today!"

"Maybe I'll get earrings to match my bracelet!" Marcy said excitedly.

Nancy, Bess, and George were silent as their friends walked toward the playground.

"I have to go to the ice-skating rink now," Bess said in a small voice.

"To practice?" George asked.

"No," Bess said. "To *quit*!"

Nancy felt bad for Bess. Skating with Alexi and Svetlana was her dream—Nancy couldn't let Deirdre spoil it!

"Deirdre is not a fortune-teller," Nancy said with a firm voice. "And the Clue Crew is going to prove it!"

"How are we going to prove it?" Bess asked.

"By finding out what *really* happened to Sherlock, that's how," Nancy said with a smile.

"Another mystery!" George cheered. She pumped her fist in the air. "Bring it on!"

Nancy looked at Bess. She didn't seem excited. Just worried. "Bess?" she asked slowly. "We're not the Clue Crew without you too."

Bess giggled at the rhyme. "Okay. I'm in," she said.

"Cool!" Nancy said. "The Clue Crew is on the case!"

The girls were about to high-five when—*whap!* A snowball hit a nearby tree. As it exploded, sticky yellow stuff dripped down the trunk!

"Ewww!" Bess said. "What is that?"

"It looks like egg," Nancy said, scrunching up her nose. "I think that snowball had a raw egg inside."

"Look out!" George shouted.

Another snowball whizzed over Nancy's head. It burst on the ground, splattering egg all over the snow. The girls ducked as more eggy snowballs flew by fast and furiously.

"It's an attack!" Bess cried.

Nancy tried to see through the whirl of snow and eggs. The egg-balls seemed to be coming from behind a snow-covered bench!

George was about to make her own snowball when—*thwack!* One exploded on the sleeve of her parka!

"Gross!" George said. She watched as sticky egg yolk dripped down her sleeve. "I am never eating scrambled eggs again!"

The icky snowballs finally stopped. The girls waited until they were sure the coast was clear. Then they walked slowly and carefully to the bench.

Nancy peeked behind it. A half-empty carton of eggs lay on the ground. Next to the box were letters carved into the snow.

"It looks like a message!" Nancy said.

The girls hurried around the bench. Nancy read the message out loud. It said:

"Gotcha! The Snowman!"

# CHAPTER FOUR

## Cold Case

"A snowman did this?" Bess cried. "Maybe it was Sherlock!"

"How could Sherlock be so mean?" George asked. "We gave him a smile!"

"But a broccoli nose!" Bess added. "No wonder he wants to get even with us."

"Oh, so now it's my fault?" George demanded.

"You guys, you guys!" Nancy said. "It might not be a *real* snowman!"

"Then who is it?" George asked.

"I don't know," Nancy said. "But we'll find out."

"I thought we were going to look for Sherlock!" Bess said.

"The pest who threw those eggs could have knocked down Sherlock too," Nancy explained. "So let's start looking for clues."

The girls squatted down to study the message. Nancy found some woolly green threads inside the letters.

"The person who wrote the message must have been wearing something green," Nancy said. She carefully picked up two threads. Then she dropped them into one of the plastic bags she always carried around "in case of a case."

Bess pointed to the message. "Look at the letter S," she said. "It's written in a curly way. Like a snake."

George found footprints leading away from the message. They were smaller than the

ones near Sherlock. And instead of a diamond design, they had a starry design on the soles.

Nancy and George wanted to look for more clues. But Bess had other plans. She had to practice for the ice show that afternoon.

"Can we watch?" George asked excitedly. "I'd love to see Alexi and Svetlana Dubonov skate!"

"And Bess Marvin!" Nancy added quickly.

The girls hooked arms and walked through the snow. On the way out of the park they saw Marcy's little sister Cassidy. The six-year-old was lying on her back making snow angels. As she waved her arms up and down, she sang at the top of her lungs: "I'm getting a puppy! A cute little puppy!"

Nancy, Bess, and George stood over Cassidy.

"Did your parents say you can have a puppy?" Nancy asked.

"No, silly!" Cassidy said. "Madame Chocolata said I'd get one."

Nancy groaned under her breath. Madame

Chocolata! Madame Chocolata! Madame Chocolata!

"Not everyone believes in Madame Chocolata, you know," Nancy said as they kept walking.

"Oh, yeah?" George said. She pointed to a long line of kids outside Deirdre's tent. They were all chanting, "We want Madame Chocolata! We want Madame Chocolata!"

Nancy stared at the crowd. Then she shrugged her shoulders and said, "So they want hot chocolate. Big deal."

Nancy and George got permission to watch Bess practice. An hour later Mrs. Marvin drove the girls to the ice-skating rink in her red van. As Mrs. Marvin parked on River Street, Nancy glanced out the window. She saw Toby Leo standing in front of the Toys 4 You store. His nose was pressed against the glass window as he gazed at the new sleds.

*Maybe Madame Chocolata told him he'd get a new sled,* Nancy thought glumly.

Inside the rink Nancy and George sat on

the bottom bleacher. They cheered for Bess as she skated out on the ice. She wasn't wearing her costume yet—just a pair of pink sweats. Svetlana and Alexi skated out to meet Bess. They were wearing matching black and silver bodysuits. Still skating, Alexi lifted Svetlana way over his head!

"There they are," Nancy whispered.

"They are so awesome!" George said.

Alexi and Svetlana skated over to Bess.

"Today we practice as if we're in the show!" Svetlana announced with a Russian accent.

"Hit music!" Alexi called out.

The song "Winter Wonderland" blared through the loudspeakers. Svetlana, Bess, and Alexi held hands as they glided across the ice.

"I can't believe Bess is skating with Svetlana and Alexi Dubonov!" George whispered.

Nancy turned to George and said, "And she hasn't fallen once!"

"Whoooaaaa!"

Nancy turned her head just in time to see

Bess sliding across the ice on her bottom!

"Oh, noooo!" Nancy cried.

"Stop music! Stop music!" Alexi shouted.

Bess slid to a stop but didn't stand up. She just sat on the ice with her head bowed.

"Don't worry, Bess," Svetlana said.

"Even we fall sometimes!" Alexi said. He pointed to his knee. "See? Hole in tights!"

Bess forced a little smile. She let Svetlana and Alexi help her to her feet.

Mrs. Marvin sat on the bleacher behind Nancy and George. "Oh, dear," she said. "Bess must be a bit nervous."

George leaned over to Nancy. "Or she's thinking about what Madame Chocolata told her," she whispered.

Nancy nodded sadly.

The ice show was in three days. If they were going to find out what happened to Sherlock, they would have to find out *fast*!

# CHAPTER FIVE

## Pranks a Lot!

"I'm such a loser," Bess said. "Maybe I should get training wheels for my skates! Or maybe Alexi and Svetlana should carry me onto the ice instead. Like a big baby!"

It was Thursday morning. The park was still covered with snow as the girls made their way through the main gate.

"You're not a loser or a baby, Bess," Nancy said. "You were just nervous."

"Sure!" George said. "I'd be nervous too if I had to skate with stars like Svetlana and Alexi. And if hundreds of people were watching me."

"Gee, thanks," Bess groaned. "I feel much better now!"

"Make way for the great Madame Chocolata!" a voice declared.

Nancy turned and saw Toby walking into the park. He was dragging the rolled-up purple and gold tent. Walking a few steps behind him was Deirdre. They were both dressed in their turbans and capes.

"There she is," George whispered. "The Marshmallow Medium!"

Nancy saw a white picnic cooler in Deirdre's hand, probably filled with hot chocolate, cups, and marshmallows.

Nancy was about to say hi when two kids ran over.

"It's her! It's Madame Chocolata!" a girl said.

"Madame Chocolata—you rock!" said a boy.

"Thank you, thank you," Deirdre said. She held up her hand. "But no autographs, please!"

As the kids walked away, Deirdre turned to Nancy, Bess, and George. Her eyes flashed with excitement.

"Do you believe it? Almost all of my fortunes

are coming true!" Deirdre squealed. "And I only became Madame Chocolata because I wanted kids to read my website. Now I'm totally famous—like a rock star!"

*Give me a break*, Nancy thought. She hoped Bess and George wouldn't tell Deirdre about their missing snowman. It would just give her another reason to brag!

"What do you think of Madame Chocolata fortune cookies?" Deirdre asked. "They would be chocolate-flavored fortune cookies, of course—"

"Whoa!" Toby shouted. "Check it out!"

Nancy looked to see where Toby was pointing. A few feet away were some bushes wrapped with white toilet paper. The kids walked over to the bushes to check them out.

"It looks like some kind of prank," George said.

A note was stuck to a branch. It was written in green ink. Nancy pulled it off and read it to herself. She blinked and read it again to make sure it was right.

"Nancy! What does it say?" Bess asked.

"It says," Nancy said slowly, "'That's a wrap! The Snowman.'"

"The Snowman again!" Bess gasped.

"What Snowman?" Deirdre asked.

"Um," Nancy said. "Er . . ."

Nancy wanted to change the subject, so she was happy to see their friends Kendra Jackson and Nadine Nardo walking by. But Kendra and Nadine looked sad as they pulled sleds covered with sticky green Silly String.

"Why did you squirt Silly String all over your sleds?" Deirdre asked. "Is it a cool new look?"

"We didn't do it," Kendra grumbled.

"Kendra and I left our sleds by a tree while we made snow angels," Nadine explained. "When we came back for our sleds they looked like this!"

"Do you know who did it?" Nancy asked.

Kendra shrugged and said, "Some weird message was written in the snow with pebbles. It said, 'The Snowman Was Here.'"

"No way!" George exclaimed. "The Snowman struck again!"

"And I'll bet he's Sherlock!" Bess said.

"Sherlock?" Deirdre asked. "You mean that snowman you built yesterday?"

Nancy raised her eyebrow at Bess as if to say, "Don't tell her." But Bess was already babbling on. . . .

"Our snowman did take a journey just like you said, Madame Chocolata," Bess said. "And now he's making trouble in the park!"

"Cool!" Deirdre exclaimed.

"What's so cool about that?" Nancy asked.

"It means another one of my fortunes came

true!" Deirdre said. "The great Madame Chocolata scores again!"

"Yeah," Toby said. He sagged from the weight of the tent. "Scores again."

Deirdre and Toby left to set up the tent. Nadine and Kendra turned to the girls with angry eyes.

"Who did you build anyway?" Nadine asked. "Frosty's evil twin?"

"You built him," Kendra said. "Now you *stop* him."

Kendra and Nadine huffed away with their sleds.

"Wow," George said. "We didn't build a snowman. We created a Frankenstein."

Nancy didn't get it. How could both her friends believe their snowman was alive? How could they believe in Madame Chocolata?

"Come on, Clue Crew," Nancy said. "Let's find out who's *really* making all this trouble. And I'll bet it's not Sherlock!"

The girls went back to work. They found more green threads on the bushes. As Bess and

George picked them up, Nancy gazed thoughtfully in the distance.

*This really is a mystery,* Nancy thought. *Who could the Snowman be?*

Suddenly something big and white dashed out from behind a tree. A bright blue scarf fluttered from its neck as it darted from tree to tree.

"Yikes!" Nancy gasped.

"Nancy—are you okay?" Bess asked.

"Yeah," George said. "You look like you just saw a ghost!"

# ChaPTeR Six

## Snowman or No-man?

Nancy gulped.

She wasn't sure *what* she saw. So she decided to keep the snowman part to herself.

"I think I saw . . . a giant white squirrel," Nancy blurted. "Yeah, that's it."

Bess and George exchanged looks.

"A giant white squirrel?" Bess repeated.

"Was he carrying a giant nut?" George chuckled.

Nancy shook her head and smiled. "I think my eyes played a trick on me," she said. "Let's go to our detective headquarters and sort out our clues."

"Good idea," Bess said. "It's so cold my face feels like it fell asleep!"

As they walked away, Nancy glanced over her shoulder at the trees. She didn't see anything big, white, and blue this time.

*All this talk about walking snowmen,* Nancy thought. *No wonder I imagined it!*

Bess stopped at a garbage can. It was filled with bright pink papers.

"Hey!" Bess said, looking inside. "These are for the Ice Spectacular Show. But what are they doing in a garbage can?"

"Come on, Bess," George said, tugging her cousin's arm. "We may be detectives, but we can't figure everything out."

Nancy, Bess, and George were happy

to reach the toasty-warm Drew house. When Hannah saw the shivering girls she poured three bowls of steaming-hot tomato soup.

"What did you girls do in the park today?" Hannah asked. "Build a snowman?"

Nancy, Bess, and George sat around the kitchen table eating their soup.

"We built a snowman two days ago," Nancy said.

"Now we're trying to find him," George said.

"Find him?" Hannah said. "Do you think he melted?"

"No," Nancy, Bess, and George said together.

"Well, then," Hannah chuckled. "He couldn't have just up and walked away!"

The girls exchanged looks around the table.

"Um," Nancy said slowly. "May we have some crackers, please?"

After lunch the girls hurried up to Nancy's room. George sat at Nancy's computer to start a new detective file. She named it "What Happened to Sherlock?" Nancy and Bess carefully

placed the green threads and the note into the clue drawer in Nancy's desk.

"I still don't get it," Bess said. "If somebody knocked down Sherlock, what happened to his things? Like his scarf, his boots, the dog kibbles, and the broccoli nose?"

"The guilty person probably took them," Nancy decided. "Or hid them somewhere."

"Poor Sherlock," George said, sighing as she typed. "Such an awesome snowman—totally wiped out!"

Wiped out? Wipeout!

"Remember the kid on the snowboard?" Nancy asked. "He yelled 'wipeout' before he almost knocked down Sherlock."

"But he *didn't* knock him down," Bess said.

"He could have come back to finish the job!" Nancy said. "If only we knew his name so we could find him."

"Maybe he goes to our school," George said. "He looked like he could have been in fourth grade."

Nancy didn't know many kids in fourth grade. But she did know her good friend Ned Nickerson!

"I'll ask Ned!" Nancy said. "He knows everybody!"

George stood up so Nancy could sit down at the computer. Nancy clicked the mouse and went online. As she scrolled down her buddy list she saw Ned's screen name. He was online too!

Bess and George peered over Nancy's shoulder as she sent Ned an instant message: "Hi Ned. Do U know a fourth grader who snowboards in the park?"

The girls waited for Ned's answer. After a few seconds they heard a chime. Ned's message popped up on the screen:

"Bradley Sorensen. He's bad news!"

"Bad news? Sounds like our man!" George said.

Nancy IM'd Ned again: "How can I find him?"

"Send him an IM," Ned sent back. "His screen name is easy 2 remember."

"What is it?" Nancy typed. She waited for Ned's message. When it popped up the girls stared at the screen. Bradley's screen name was—

"The Snowman!" Nancy gasped.

# CHAPTER SEVEN

## Chill on the Hill

"That's the name we found at the scenes of the crimes," George exclaimed. "Bradley's got to be guilty!"

"Go ahead, Nancy!" Bess said. She pointed to the keyboard. "Send Bradley an instant message!"

Nancy thanked Ned and signed off. "I think I'd rather question Bradley face to face first," she said. "If we can find him again."

"We can look for Bradley in the park," George said.

Nancy thought about Bradley's fancy moves on his snowboard. "Or we can look for him somewhere else," she said.

"Where?" Bess and George asked together.

"Nightmare Hill!" Nancy said with a grin.

"Whoa!" George cried. "That's the steepest hill in River Heights!"

"You have to be superbrave to go down Nightmare Hill," Bess said. "Or supercrazy!"

Nancy thought of Bradley and said, "Exactly!"

Nightmare Hill was five blocks away. The girls had permission to walk there together. As they stood on the hilltop they saw a few extreme sledders and snowboarders. But not Bradley.

"I guess even Bradley's not crazy enough to go down Nightmare Hill." Nancy sighed.

They were about to walk away when someone yelled, "King of the hill! I'm king of the hill! Woo-hooooo!"

Nancy whipped around. Zipping down the hill on his snowboard was Bradley Sorensen. He was wearing black ski goggles, a blue parka, and matching pants. Suddenly Nancy noticed something else. . . .

"Look at Bradley's gloves!" Nancy said. "They're

green—the same color as those
woolly threads we found!"

"I told you he was guilty!"
George said.

"Not yet," Nancy said.
"There's one more thing I
want to find out."

Bradley began
climbing back up
the hill.

"Bradley Sorensen!"
Nancy called. "I
can't believe it!
Can I have your
autograph? Can I? Can I?"

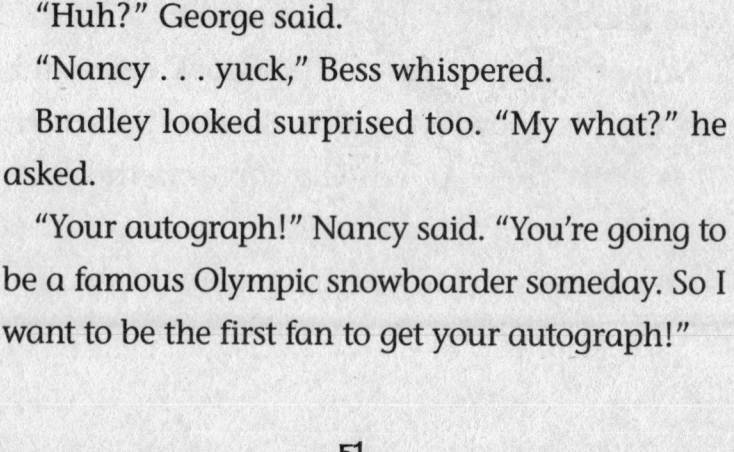

"Huh?" George said.

"Nancy . . . yuck," Bess whispered.

Bradley looked surprised too. "My what?" he
asked.

"Your autograph!" Nancy said. "You're going to
be a famous Olympic snowboarder someday. So I
want to be the first fan to get your autograph!"

"I think I'm going to barf," George muttered.

Bradley grinned. He reached into his pocket and pulled out an empty candy bar wrapper. Then he pulled out a pen. Nancy watched as Bradley scribbled his name on the wrapper.

"Here," Bradley said. He held out the wrapper. "But next time I charge five bucks!"

Nancy snatched the wrapper. She looked at the autograph and shouted—

"Just as I thought. Green ink!"

Bess jabbed the autograph.

"And look!" she said. "The letter S is curly. The same as the messages!"

"What are you girlies talking about?" Bradley cried.

"You're the one who did all those mean pranks in the park," Nancy said. "You're the Snowman!"

Bradley narrowed his eyes at the girls. Then he slipped his feet into his snowboard and said, "Oh, yeah? Catch me if you can!"

The girls watched as Bradley pushed down the hill.

"Oh, great," George said. "He's getting away!"

Bess glanced around. She ran over to a big sheet of cardboard and dragged it over.

"What's that?" Nancy asked.

"An instant sled," Bess said. "Hop on!"

"But this is Nightmare Hill!" George cried. They sat in a row on the cardboard. Then they leaned forward and pushed it down the hill!

"Whoaaaaaaaa!" the girls shouted.

Nancy gritted her teeth as they sped after Bradley. It was like being on the bumpiest, scariest roller-coaster ride!

"King of the hill!" Bradley shouted as he gained speed. "King of the—aaaaaaah!"

Bradley's snowboard flipped over. He flew through the air and landed right in a snowbank.

The cardboard sled stopped at the bottom of the hill. The girls jumped off and ran to Bradley. He was standing up covered with snow.

"Now you're king of the *spill*!" George laughed.

"Why did you do it, Bradley?" Nancy asked. "Why did you do all those pranks?"

"I don't know what you're talking about!" Bradley growled.

Bradley dusted himself off. Suddenly Nancy spotted something stuck to his sleeve. It looked like a strand of green Silly String!

"I think you *do* know what I'm talking about," Nancy said. She plucked the string from his sleeve and smiled.

Bradley stared at the string and sighed.

"Okay, so I squirted a bunch of sleds," he said. "And papered some bushes. And threw some eggs. Big deal!"

"You forgot something," George said. "You knocked down our snowman too."

"No way!" Bradley said. "That I didn't do!"

"You didn't?" Nancy asked.

"Nah!" Bradley said. "I stopped knocking down snowmen in second grade!"

Bradley picked up his board. Then he stomped his way up the hill.

"How do we know he's telling the truth?" Bess asked.

George pointed to one of Bradley's footprints.

"His boots have that starry design on the sole," George said. "Just like the footprints near the pranks."

"But not like the ones near Sherlock," Bess said.

"I don't think Bradley knocked down Sherlock," Nancy said. "And he won't make any more trouble either now that we know who the Snowman is."

"But we still don't know what happened to Sherlock," George said.

Nancy, Bess, and George chatted as they walked away from the hill. The friends still couldn't believe they had sledded down the highest hill in River Heights!

"And I built a sled!" Bess said proudly. "Well . . . sort of!"

The girls headed back to the Drew house. Nancy's puppy Chocolate Chip was tethered to a tree in the front yard. The chain fastened to Chip's collar was long enough for her to romp around in the snow.

Chip buried her little brown face in the snow. When she pulled it out, it was completely white!

"Chip loves the snow!" Nancy said.

"I can see that!" George laughed.

Inside the house the girls sat around the

kitchen table drinking Hannah's yummy hot chocolate. They forgot all about the case as they giggled and licked chocolate mustaches from their lips. As they sipped their last drops Hannah held out Chip's leash.

"Now that you've had some hot chocolate," Hannah said, "how about walking Chocolate Chip?"

Nancy, Bess, and George bundled up again and went outside. Chip's chain was still attached to the tree. But Chip was gone!

Nancy's heart beat faster and faster. "B-Bess, George!" she stammered. "Somebody took my dog!"

# ChaPTER Eight

## Chip, Chip, Hooray!

Nancy was about to shout for Hannah when she heard a bark. She ran onto the sidewalk and looked down the street. A boy was carrying Chip away!

"It looks like Toby Leo!" Nancy said.

"What's he doing with Chip?" Bess asked.

Chip's ears flopped up and down as Toby hurried down the block. "Toby—stop!" Nancy shouted.

Toby looked over his shoulder. His mouth dropped open when he saw the girls. Chip barked. As she jumped out of Toby's arms she dragged the scarf off his neck.

"Sorry, Nancy!" Toby called as he ran away. "I didn't mean it! Honest!"

The girls raced over to Chip. Nancy scooped her up and held her tight. She attached Chip's leash to her puppy's collar.

"Why would Toby take Chip?" Nancy asked.

"Maybe he wanted a puppy," Bess said with a shrug. "Everybody wants a cute little puppy."

Nancy thought of Cassidy making snow angels and singing about a puppy. That's when it began to click.

"Didn't Madame Chocolata tell Cassidy she would get a puppy?" Nancy asked.

"Yeah, so?" George said.

"Maybe Toby took Chip to give to Cassidy!" Nancy said. "So it would look like Deirdre's fortune came true!"

"Maybe Toby is making *all* of Madame Chocolata's fortunes come true!" George said. "Like Marcy's bracelet. And Trina's basketball—"

"And Sherlock!" Bess gasped.

Nancy picked up the scarf. It had a tiny hole at the end, just like the one she had wrapped around Sherlock.

"Toby lives right around the corner," Nancy said. She tied the scarf around her own neck. "Let's see what we can find out."

The Clue Crew walked Chip around the corner to the Leo house. George rang the doorbell. When no one answered they headed around

the house to the backyard. There was a swing set and a snow-covered picnic table.

But no Toby.

Just then Chip tugged at her leash. The little puppy pulled Nancy in the direction of a tree.

"What is it, girl?" Nancy asked.

"Maybe she has to go again," George said.

But when Chip stopped at the tree she started digging. She dug and dug until she reached something in the snow. Nancy could see they were little round dog kibbles.

"Bess, George, look!" Nancy said. "Those are the same kind of kibbles we used for Sherlock's nose and mouth!"

"What else is down there?" George asked.

While Chip munched on the kibbles, the girls brushed away more snow. Buried underneath was a pair of old rubber boots.

"My dad's boots!" George exclaimed.

Nancy picked one up. It felt heavy. She tipped it over and a stalk of broccoli and earmuffs spilled out!

"Those are the earmuffs I made for Sherlock!" Bess cried. "And that's his broccoli nose!"

Nancy scratched Chip behind her ears. "Good girl, Chip!" she said. "You found some awesome clues. And I think we found the person who knocked down Sherlock!"

Nancy hurried to bring Chip home. Then the Clue Crew marched straight to the park.

They walked past a long line of kids in front of Madame Chocolata's tent.

"Hey! Wait your turn!" a boy shouted out.

"Quit jumping the line!" a girl said.

"Um—we're delivering marshmallows," George said quickly. "Can't tell fortunes without marshmallows!"

The girls slipped inside the tent. Deirdre and Toby were sitting on the blanket counting dollar bills.

"Fifteen, sixteen," Toby counted. "Seventeen—"

"Toby Leo!" Nancy snapped.

"Wha!" Toby cried. The dollars flew out of his hands as he jumped up. "Nancy! I-I g-gave you back your dog!"

"What's up?" Deirdre asked. "I mean—what

can Madame Chocolata tell you today?"

"How about telling us if Toby knocked down our snowman," Nancy said.

"Tell us, Toby," George said. "Or we'll tell your parents that you took Nancy's dog right out of her yard!"

"I told you I didn't mean to take the puppy!" Toby said. "It was temporary insanity! Temporary insanity!"

"Dog? Snowman?" Deirdre said. "What's going on?"

Toby hung his head. "Okay, okay," he said. "I've been listening in on your fortunes, Deirdre. And I've been making them come true."

"What?" Deirdre gasped.

"I knocked down their snowman," Toby went on.

"I even put on his boots and walked out of the park—so it would look like his footsteps!"

"And you buried the boots in your yard," Nancy said. "Along with the kibbles, the earmuffs, the broccoli nose—"

"But I kept the scarf!" Toby cut in. He pointed to the scarf around Nancy's neck. "Blue is my favorite color!"

"Why did you do it, Toby?" Bess asked.

"So Madame Chocolata would have lots of customers," Toby explained. "We were splitting the money even-steven. The more money I got, the more I'd have to buy that new sled I wanted."

Nancy got it. No wonder Toby was staring into the toy store window yesterday.

"But I had to use all my money to buy stuff like pizzas and plastic bracelets," Toby said with a frown. "I even gave Trina Vanderhoof one of my own basketballs because I couldn't afford to buy a new one."

Deirdre glared at Toby long and hard.

"All this time I thought my fortunes were coming true!" she said between gritted teeth. "I was going to have my own fortune cookies! A new website! I was even going to write a best-selling book called *Mystic Marshmallows*!"

"Sorry, Deirdre," Toby said. "Once I started I couldn't quit. But I'll quit now. I promise!"

Deirdre reached up and pulled off her turban. "Well, if I can't tell fortunes, then I quit too!" she declared.

"What?" Nancy, Bess, and George said together.

"These hoop earrings pinch and this stupid tent is freezing," Deirdre groaned. "And if I have to stare at one more marshmallow I'll flip!"

"So you're not Madame Chocolata anymore?" Nancy asked.

"I am so over it!" Deirdre said. She turned to Bess. "I'm sorry I said you'd fall on the ice. I was just mad you called me silly."

"And I'm sorry I called you silly," Bess said.

Nancy was so happy she could do cartwheels. The Clue Crew solved the case. And Bess and Deirdre made up!

Just then the kids outside the tent began to shout.

"We want Madame Chocolata! We want

Madame Chocolata! We want Madame Chocolata!"

"Uh-oh," Nancy said. "How are you going to
tell all those kids that you quit?"

"Oh, *I'm* not telling them," Deirdre said. She
crossed her arms and turned to Toby.

"Me?" Toby squeaked.

Nancy, Bess, and George slipped out of the
tent past the crowd.

"Did you hear that?" Bess said happily.
"Deirdre made up the fortune that I'd fall in
the show!"

"And Toby confessed to knocking down Sherlock!" Nancy said. "So we solved the case!"

They were about to high-five when Nancy
saw something big and white flit by in the distance. This time Bess and George saw it too.

"Did you see that?" Bess gasped. "It looked
like a walking snowman!"

"He's back," Nancy said slowly.

"Back?" George said. "You mean you saw him
once before?"

Nancy explained how she had seen a figure that looked like a snowman. But she hadn't said anything because she wasn't sure if she saw it or not.

The girls walked carefully to where they had seen the figure, but all they could see were his footprints. They weren't like the footprints the boots had made, though. They were huge deep holes in the snow.

Nancy, Bess, and George were silent as they stared at the strange footprints.

"This case is not closed," Nancy said. "Not until we find out who that was."

"Or *what* it was," Bess said with a shiver.


That night Nancy sat in the den watching TV. She wasn't really paying attention, though. She was too busy wondering about the mysterious figure they had seen in the park that day.

*It looked like a snowman,* Nancy thought. *But was it a snowman?*

Nancy clicked the remote to surf the channels. She stopped when she saw a news reporter standing in front of the River Heights Museum of Natural History. It was Nancy's favorite museum. It even had dinosaur bones inside!

"There have been many sightings of the Yeti," the reporter said. "Also known as the Abominable Snowman."

Nancy sat up straight.

Did she say "snowman"?

# ChAPTER NiNE

## Heads Up!

Nancy turned up the sound.

"A special exhibit on the Abominable Snowman opened at the museum today," the reporter was saying. "So come in and enjoy rare pictures of the famous walking snowman!"

"Walking snowman?" Nancy gasped. "Omigosh!"

Nancy raced to find her father. Mr. Drew was sitting at the kitchen table paying bills.

"Daddy, Daddy?" Nancy asked. "Did you ever hear of the Abominable Snowman?"

"Sure have," Mr. Drew said. "I think he's also called Bigfoot."

"Bigfoot!" Nancy gasped under her breath.

She remembered the footprints they saw in the snow. They were big. Very big!

"Daddy, can I please call George?" Nancy asked. "It's about our case."

"Sure," Mr. Drew said. "Just don't stay on too long."

Nancy ran back to the den. She picked up the phone and quickly dialed George's number.

"Fayne residence and catering service," George said as she answered. "Who is speaking—"

"George, call Bess!" Nancy cut in. "We're going to the Museum of Natural History first thing tomorrow!"

That night Nancy tossed and turned in bed. She couldn't stop wondering if the snowman they had seen in the park was the Abominable Snowman. Or Bigfoot!

*Maybe I should have taken a picture too,* Nancy said as she slowly drifted off to sleep.

The next day was Friday. Right after breakfast Hannah drove Nancy, Bess, and George to the

museum. While Hannah admired an exhibit on rare gems, the girls checked out the Abominable Snowman exhibit. The director of the museum, Mr. Fauntelroy, pointed out all of the photographs.

"Are you sure that's the Abominable Snowman?" Nancy asked. "It looks more like some furry ape!"

Nancy tilted her head as she studied one of the pictures. It showed a white furry creature lumbering through the woods. His arms hung low and his feet were flat and long.

"Well, now," Mr. Fauntelroy said. His mustache wiggled as he spoke. "What did you expect the

Abominable Snowman to look like?"

George shrugged and said, "The snowman we saw in the park had a blue scarf around his neck!"

"And he was kind of cute," Bess said. "In a roly-poly way."

Mr. Fauntelroy blinked. He cracked a small smile and said, "I don't think you saw the Abominable Snowman, girls. I think you had a *Frosty* sighting!"

Nancy smiled politely as Mr. Fauntelroy laughed at his own joke. She knew they hadn't seen Frosty the Snowman. And she knew they hadn't seen Bigfoot either.

"Thanks for showing us the pictures, Mr. Fauntelroy," Nancy said. "They were very interesting."

"You're welcome!" Mr. Fauntelroy said. "And don't forget about our insect exhibit in the spring. We'll have one of the world's biggest cockroaches under glass!"

"Ew," Bess said as they walked away.

The girls joined Hannah in the gem room. She was only halfway through the exhibit.

"Why don't you girls look for your birth-stones?" she said. "There's supposed to be a giant amethyst around here."

"I think we'd rather talk about our case now, Hannah," Nancy said.

"Okay, Clue Crew," Hannah said with a smile. "Meet me outside in fifteen minutes. Stay by the entrance and don't go anywhere."

Nancy, Bess, and George bundled up in their jackets, scarves, and hats. They walked through the revolving door and stood outside on the sidewalk.

"The snowman we saw in the park wasn't the Abominable Snowman," Nancy sighed.

"I guess it's back to square one," George said.

Bess stared at the River Heights Ice-Skating Rink. It was right next to the museum.

"The ice show is tomorrow!" Bess said. "I have my costume. I know what I have to do. So why am I so nervous?"

"It's okay, Bess," Nancy said. "I'll bet even Svetlana and Alexi Dubonov are nervous about the show."

Suddenly Bess's eyes popped wide open. "Omigosh! Omigosh! Omigosh!" she cried.

"Not *that* nervous!" George said.

"No!" Bess cried. Her finger shook as she pointed over Nancy's and George's shoulders. "It's him! It's him! It's the snowman!"

Nancy and George whipped around. The snowman they had seen in the park was running across the street.

"Cheese and crackers—it is him!" George exclaimed.

Nancy stared at the snowman as his scarf flapped in the wind. In his hands were some bright pink papers.

"What are we waiting for?" George said. She started to run. "Let's go after him!"

Nancy grabbed the hem of George's jacket. "We can't!" she said. "Hannah told us to wait here!"

The girls shouted after the snowman.

"Stop!" Nancy yelled.

"Freeze!" George shouted. "I mean—thaw!"

The snowman kept dashing down River Street.

George bent down and scooped up a handful of snow. "They didn't make me pitcher on our baseball team for nothing," she said. "Stand back!"

George patted the snow into a snowball. She swung back her arm and hurled it across the street. It hit the snowman on the shoulder with a loud *thonk!*

"Got him!" George cheered.

The top part of the snowman toppled off. Nancy watched in horror as it rolled over and over on the icy ground.

"You did more than that, George!" Nancy cried. "You knocked off his head!"

# CHAPTER TEN

## Nice on Ice

The girls stared across the street. In place of the snowman's head was a human head. A teenage boy's head!

"It's a costume," George said.

The boy kneeled down to pick up the pink papers.

"What goes on here?" a voice with a Russian accent demanded.

Nancy, Bess, and George turned around. Standing at the stage door of the ice rink were Svetlana and Alexi Dubonov!

"We heard noise and come out!" Alexi said. He and Svetlana wrapped themselves in their coats as they walked over to the girls.

"Bess, is everything good?" Svetlana asked.

"I think so," Bess said.

Nancy's mouth hung wide open. She couldn't believe they were actually standing next to the famous ice-skaters. Her voice shook as she pointed and said, "Um—we saw that snowman across the street. I mean we saw him before, in the park!"

Alexi looked across the street and said, "That is Lance. He hands out fliers for the show in front of the rink."

"Oh!" Bess said. "Just like those fliers we saw in the garbage can!"

"Garbage can?" Alexi and Svetlana said together.

Lance walked across the street with his snowman head under his arm. "Yo," he said. "Who threw that snowball?"

"I did," George admitted.

Nancy expected Lance to be mad, but instead he smiled.

"Wicked pitch!" Lance said with a grin. "You go, girl!"

"Thanks!" George said, grinning back.

But Alexi and Svetlana were not smiling.

"What were you doing in the park, Lance?" Alexi asked. "When you should have been giving out fliers here?"

Lance's face turned red. It wasn't from the cold!

"I didn't know I'd have to dress up like a snowman when I took the job," Lance said. "If my buds saw me like this they'd be on my case for weeks."

"But you were a great snowman," Nancy said. "You really had us fooled!"

"And there's nothing wrong with wearing a snowman suit," Bess said.

"There is if you're the star of your high-school ice hockey team," Lance said. He turned to Svetlana and Alexi. "I'm sorry about the fliers. I'll work extra late tonight to hand them out."

But Svetlana looked deep in thought. "Ice hockey?" she said. "You skate, Lance?"

"Like a pro!" Lance admitted. "The team calls me Lance the Blade!"

Svetlana turned to Nancy and George. "Do you skate too?" she asked.

"We love to skate!" Nancy said.

"I even did a figure eight once!" George said. "Well . . . it was more like a figure six. But close enough."

Svetlana turned to her husband and smiled. "Lance skate. Girls skate," she said. "Alexi—I have a huge idea!"

Nancy traded puzzled looks with Bess and George. What could it be?

"You were awesome in the ice show, Bess," Nancy said.

"And I didn't fall once!" Bess said happily.

It was Saturday night. Bess had just skated with Svetlana and Alexi in the River Heights Ice Spectacular Show. Thanks to the skating couple, Nancy and George had parts too. They wore colorful snowsuits and skated out on the ice with Lance the Snowman!

This time Lance didn't mind wearing a

snowman suit. Especially when his hockey team started cheering, "Go Blade! Go Blade! Go Blade!"

After the show the Drews, Faynes, and Marvins went to Pizza Paradise for pies all around. But Nancy, Bess, and George celebrated more than just the ice show. They celebrated one more mystery solved by the Clue Crew!

"Large pepperoni pizza with cheese!" the perky waitress with the ponytail said. She

placed the pie on the small round table the girls shared. "Enjoy your meal!"

Nancy waited for the waitress to walk away. Then she closed her eyes and began waving both hands over the pie.

"Nancy!" George whispered. Her eyes darted around to see if anyone was looking. "What are you doing?"

"I am Madame Pepperona!" Nancy said with a deep voice. "And I read pepperonis on pizza pies!"

Bess giggled and said, "So what do you see in our future, Madame Pepperona?"

Nancy opened her eyes and smiled. "Mysteries!" she said. "Lots and lots of mysteries!"

# Make a Snowflake!

There's no business like snow business! But you don't have to live in a snowy state like Nancy, Bess, and George to have fun with flakes. Just get crafty—and make your own!

Beaded snowflakes are pretty and fun to make!

## *You will need:

Gold, white, or silver pipe cleaners (three
for each snowflake)
One sunburst bead for the middle of
each snowflake
Lots of beads—white, clear,
crystal, or pastel
Glue and glitter
String
(*You can pick up most snowflake supplies
at a local crafts store!)

## Ready, Set, Snow . . .

Take three pipe cleaners and your sunburst bead. Stick the pipe cleaners through the hole of the sunburst bead so they are the same length on each side of the bead. Spread the pipe cleaners out to make the frame of the snowflake. Add beads to pipe cleaners. When pipe cleaner is filled with beads, fold the end into the last bead. For extra shimmer, dot your snowflake with glue and sprinkle on glitter! No two snowflakes are alike, so go wild with different shapes and designs!

To hang up your snowflake, tie a thin or see-through string to the top. Or to make a sassy "snow mobile" for your room, hang a bunch of snowflakes on the frame of a coat hanger!

# A Frosty Fact!

All snowflakes may be different, but they have one thing in common: They all have six sides and six points!

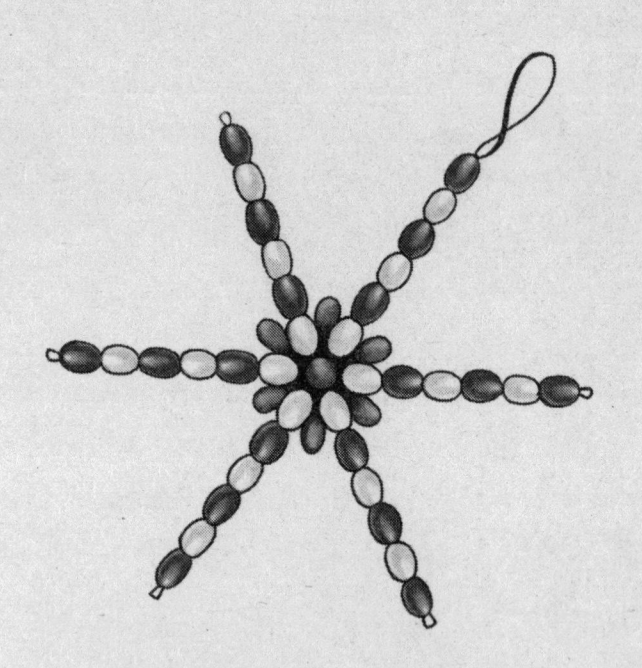